DARE TO LC

The Dare Series 4

Dixie Lynn Dwyer

MENAGE EVERLASTING

Siren Publishing, Inc.
www.SirenPublishing.com

A SIREN PUBLISHING BOOK
IMPRINT: Ménage Everlasting

DARE TO LOVE
Copyright © 2016 by Dixie Lynn Dwyer

ISBN: 978-1-63259-865-3

First Printing: May 2016

Cover design by Les Byerley
All art and logo copyright © 2016 by Siren Publishing, Inc.

Printed in the U.S.A.

PUBLISHER
Siren Publishing, Inc.
www.SirenPublishing.com

DEDICATION

Dear readers,

Thank you for purchasing this legal copy of Dare to Love.

Mercedes has known hardship, sacrifice and hard work all her life. She's witnessed loved ones die, learned to fend for herself and survive on the necessities.

As she struggles with letting her guard down and opening her heart, she picks the wrong moment, the wrong men, and it nearly costs her everything.

But despite thinking that three certain men aren't interested in her as anything more than as friends, it's proven otherwise as two of them rescue her and save her from a dreadful fate.

But she isn't out of danger. She's also not too sure she can handle falling for three men when she's more scared than ever before.

May you enjoy Mercedes's journey. Will she dare to love Kurt, Taylor and Warner, or will it be too late when she finally realizes that love is indeed very powerful, especially in a town like Chance?

Happy reading.
Hugs!

~Dixie~

DARE TO LOVE

The Dare Series 4

DIXIE LYNN DWYER
Copyright © 2016

Prologue

"We could really use your help, Kurt. You and Warner know so much about security systems, monitoring and securing large venues, and my brothers and I trust you guys. We've been friends forever," Jack Spencer said to Kurt Dawn as they stood by the bar.

Kurt looked around the place, then back toward Jack. Jack wondered what his friend was thinking.

"You really don't need such high-tech security here, Jack. Some of the basic systems will do, and during business hours, you need reliable security staff. You know this already. You and Danny have a great system that your employees already know," Kurt replied as he looked back down at his beer.

His friend was down as usual. He and his brother Warner were retired government men. They did some mercenary work amongst other things that they never shared. Jack had a feeling it was weighing its toll on them and they wanted out. Maybe convincing them to run his whole security here at Spencer's would be a motivator?

"The place is going to be a lot bigger now, Kurt. You know as well as I do that a bigger place brings in people from all over. I've got Max on my ass about security being of the highest standards, and to be honest, it's overwhelming. Marlena's helping out a bunch, too, but to be honest, we haven't exactly been able to spend the quality time we need to be spending together because we're all stressed out. When Danny and I think about running security besides everything else like the orders, the staff, training a manager, it's just too much to have to worry about security. If you and Warner were interested, it would give us peace of mind. We trust you. There are some shady characters out there."

Kurt nodded his head as he looked around the place again.

"Warner is out of town on business. Let me talk to him when he gets back at the end of the week. We're supposed to be retired, but that really hasn't happened. Sometimes I think we're busier than ever."

"This could be a good change for you guys. Plus your brother Taylor wouldn't be so on edge when the two of you are away on 'business' as you like to call it."

Kurt raised one of his eyebrows at Jack.

"Listen, I'm not prying. I respect that your jobs are secretive and that they're very dangerous. I know Taylor's been itching to settle down and maybe start a family."

"We all are on the same page with that. But transitioning to civilians, ending our government careers for good, is a heavy decision and a huge step."

"We'll pay you both a great salary, so you'll have income," Jack added.

Kurt gave him a look.

"You know money isn't a problem for us, right?" he replied. Jack nodded his head and gave a smirk. He knew damn well that money wasn't a problem for the Dawn men. Whatever they did for a living, they made a lot of money. But no one would even notice. They dressed casual all the time, looking intense, hard, and ready for action and a fight more often than not. They were big men, physically fit, and capable of things Jack didn't even want to imagine.

"Think of the money as fun cash. You know when the three of you take a woman out on a date and go on vacation and shit. Which we'll have to work out. If you take the job," Jack added.

This time Kurt smirked.

"We'll see. Let me mull it over and talk with Warner. Our services are needed in a lot of places other than Chance."

"Well I for one and happy about that. Don't need any trouble coming this way."

"You're right, but things are changing, Jack. Even the small towns can get tainted by crime, violence, and unsuspecting people like a lot of the residents in Chance. I, for one, don't want any of them to become victims. And I understand Max's concerns. Even if Warner and I don't take the positions we'll help you out. You know, train your manager of security and make sure they have their shit together."

"Fair enough. But I hope you two accept our offer. We need you and more importantly, we trust you."

* * * *

Kurt sat at the bar thinking about Jack's offer. He turned down a few women who approached him tonight, looking for a good time. He wasn't interested. Hadn't been interested in even easing the ache he had. He knew exactly why. Taylor was feeling it, but he got to see Mercedes on a daily basis at work. Then again, that was probably torture. Then of course Warner was being the most resistant to even admitting he was interested in Mercedes. So what did he do? He took the next private job and shipped off to Cuba for a few weeks.

Kurt shook his head. Apparently he wasn't the smartest. He should have taken a trip away, too. But then he'd worry about Mercedes. It wasn't even really because she was in danger or needed the protection. It was the fact that he liked protecting her. He liked being close to her and smelling her perfume or that delicious shampoo that was all Mercedes.

Fuck me.

He tried to force the thoughts from his head and looked around at the crowd of people. He was pretty damn good at reading people, watching them and determining what their next moves were. His gut instincts were his greatest survival tool over the years. He never second-guessed it.

He watched several people, finding them not quite suspicious but perhaps up to no good. One particular guy, about six feet tall and stocky, kept looking around the room, as if he were making sure security weren't nearby. Sure enough, the son of a bitch pulled out a baggie with drugs and exchanged it with some woman as she passed by, pretended to bump into him, and hand over the money. It was quick, but it was sloppy. Kurt looked at the one bouncer who was nearby and sure enough he hadn't seen a thing. That was what Jack and Danny were going to need here. Security that could break up fights, control crowds, and escort drunks from the building and into cabs. They needed men who were trained for this kind of stuff. Trained to stop drugs from destroying an establishment.

As he continued to look around he caught sight of a guy lifting his cell phone and appeared to be taking pictures but he couldn't be sure. Kurt saw what the guy took a picture of. Harmless? Three young women, early twenties, all dolled up, wearing short, tight dresses and waving at a group of older men nearby. He glanced back toward the guy who'd been taking the pictures and he was gone. That was quick, he thought and then heard his name and felt the hand on his shoulder.

"There you are. I was looking for you," Taylor said as he took a seat by the bar. The bartender immediately placed down a Bud Light and Taylor took a long guzzle.

"Bad day at work?" Kurt asked and took a sip from the new bottle of beer that the bartender placed down in front of him, too.

His brother gave him that look as if he automatically knew what Taylor meant. Then it hit him. Mercedes.

He held Taylor's gaze as he took a sip of beer. Taylor looked around them and then leaned over the bar a little. He wondered why today upset his brother. Had some guy asked her out? Had she accepted? Was she feeling okay? He felt sick. This was getting worse. He put on an expressionless face and took a sip from his beer and waited for his brother to update him.

"I heard her on the phone today. That sweet, sexy voice of hers being so nice to everyone. Then when I walked up to her desk to see if she had some forms ready for me she was direct and short. 'Deputy Dawn, I will put them in your mailbox the moment I complete them. I'm on the last page now,' she said and then went right back to typing. Her phone rang and don't you know, she answered it all sweet and calm," Taylor said, sounding frustrated as he took another long slug of beer.

Kurt wanted to laugh but he knew Taylor was having a hard time not staking a claim on Mercedes. They needed to get to know her and she needed to get to know them, but every time Taylor tried to persuade her to go for coffee together she would decline. She was shy and she was resistant to all of them.

"Maybe I could have been a bit more calm and understanding months ago when Marlena was in trouble. I mean I yelled at her and told Mercedes that she had to listen to me or else. I was so upset. The things I saw Tony do in Marlena's bedroom and then when he abducted her. I was scared and worried about Mercedes," Taylor admitted.

Kurt understood. He was very angry at the time and worried about Mercedes, but he also knew he was resistant to letting down his guard and getting to know her. He rarely dated. Never found a woman to be of more interest than for sex and to ease his ache after traveling abroad and risking his life. He felt indispensable, unstoppable, inhuman at times, and then he saw Mercedes, met her, hung out with her and her friends, and things started changing. He started, too, and apparently so did his brothers.

"She understood that, Taylor. She had to understand the intensity of the situation. If not at that moment then afterwards as she heard what was left at Marlena's cottage and then what happened in the cabin. I'm glad the guy is dead."

"Me, too," Taylor told him and then they both put down their empty beers.

"When is Warner going to get back? It's been four weeks," Taylor said.

"Beats the fuck out of me. He does what he wants. Not much can hold him down," Kurt responded.

"He's running away from his feelings for Mercedes. He doesn't think he's good enough for her," Taylor whispered.

Kurt took a slug of his beer.

"Can't blame him. Sometimes I feel the same way."

"But neither of you should feel like that. You deserve to be happy. After the kind of shit you guys do for a living, this could be the opportunity to settle down and make some changes. I worry when you guys are gone on some fucking mission or whatever you call it," Taylor told him then took a slug from the new beer the bartender just put down. He looked toward the bar, appearing uncomfortable for admitting his feelings. But Kurt could read it in his brother's eyes. He worried that something would happen to Kurt and Warner.

"You're assuming that Mercedes has the same feelings and would be interested in being shared by us. You're also assuming that she as well as us will be so compatible and so into one another that she's the one. That's a lot of assumptions and you can't even get her to hang out with you never mind go on a date. I'm just not sure about all the risks."

"I hear what you're saying, Kurt, and I've been over it in my head a thousand times at least. But I keep coming back to the same thing. The simple facts when it comes to Mercedes."

"And what are those, bro?" Kurt asked then took a slug of beer.

Taylor held Kurt's gaze.

"All three of us are attracted to her. We all worry about her, keep an extra eye out on her whenever she's nearby, hell, you and Warner have gone out of your ways to be in the same places as her just so you can get a glimpse of her, maybe say hello, or just like I said, make sure that she's safe. That isn't normal behavior. It isn't being good men of Chance and watching out for one of the single women of this town. It's wanting her. Wanting to get to know her, hold her, kiss, hell, make love to her and claim her all ours. That's the difference. That's why she's special. Mark my words, she'll be ours. She'll be Mrs. Dawn. You, and especially Warner, just need to get your heads out of your asses and admit it."

Kurt didn't know how to respond to him. Anything he thought of saying would be lies, words spewed from his lips that he didn't mean and that were plain bullshit. Instead he looked away, took a sip from his beer, and thought about what Taylor said. He was right, and as soon as he worked out his personal reasons for trying to keep Mercedes at arm's distance, maybe he could take the chance, too, and be a family, just like what their mom and dads had.

Chapter 1

Mercedes was in the supermarket doing some shopping. She had her list, everything budgeted out, and even had her coupons. She had the routine down pat, and many locals had asked her how she saved so much and where she found such great coupons. They thought she was being savvy. But it was way more than that. For most of her life she was poor. Her parents were both disabled and very ill. She had been their caregiver and they were on a very fixed income. What they could save they did for her to help assist her for school. When they passed away, she was only eighteen years old. High school was just ending. Her parents hadn't lived long enough to see her graduate or to be accepted into college.

The little money they put aside for her wasn't enough to help her with school. So she took a job as a secretary in the local college campus and worked as a bartender on weekends. She sold their house and broke even. She rented an apartment and for the first year she just made the payments at the end of every month.

As Mercedes looked at the beautiful fruit and delicious salad bar, she thought about the many times she went hungry. Having one meal a day and trying to keep up the energy to work, go to school, study, and pass had been difficult to say the least. But she did it for her parents. Her only family. The two people who cried because they believed they failed her as parents.

She closed her eyes and took a deep breath. That was so many years ago. It didn't even seem real anymore. Those days, weeks, months of starving, of making ends barely met and then graduating from college.

Thank God she came to Chance. Thank God for Mrs. Peters. She had been tired of meeting the same types of men. Men that wanted sex and thought that just because they paid for a movie or a dinner date that she should put out. There weren't any good men or even good people around where she lived. Well, except for Mrs. Peters, who lived in Chance. She had been a professor for years and then she stayed on in retirement and worked in the main office alongside the dean of school.

Mercedes smiled to herself. Mrs. Peters was the one that told her about the job opening in Chance with the sheriff's department. When she'd arrived for the interview she was a nervous wreck. Max had been so intimidating. She knew he was a good man, an honest and caring man, but had a role to play and an appearance to keep up to enforce the law. She was thrilled that he and his brothers fell in love with her friend Alicia.

Mercedes smiled and continued around the store picking up the items on her list. She gathered her coupons and knew she would be right on target to her spending this week. But when she got to the floral section and saw the bright yellow bouquet of flowers and admired them, she felt that instant anxiety in her chest. They were quite beautiful. But not in her budget. She could afford to get them, now that she was working full time, but there was always that fear. That worry that if she was frivolous here and there, it could get out of control and she would be in debt again. She gulped down the lump of emotions. It made her belly ache.

She looked at the price and cringed. Not this week. She just didn't spend foolishly and really, what would she do with them? She was hardly home enough to enjoy them. She walked away and headed toward the register. She talked to Lucy, one of the teenagers that worked there, and they chatted about her brother, Gardner, a deputy. They laughed, exchanged pleasantries, and Mercedes once again felt grateful for living in a place like Chance. It was safe, people were friendly and kind, and she felt at ease, not on guard like she did years ago.

As Mercedes walked out of the store with her bags in the cart and headed to her car, she heard her cell phone ring. Glancing at the caller ID she saw that it was Marlena.

"Hi, Marlena, how are you?"

"I'm doing well, what are you up to?"

"Just finished food shopping and heading home to put it away then get back to the station. What's new?"

"You really do like to keep your time organized. I bet you had a lot of coupons. How much did you save today?"

"About twenty-five dollars. But it wasn't a big food shopping."

"That is great. You'll have to teach me so that I can be a savvy, smart shopper."

"With Danny, Jack, and Mike spoiling you the way they do, you don't need to worry."

"That they do. In fact, I'm calling you to see what you're doing on Friday night? There's a comedy show in Wager and I can get great tickets, close to the stage for the four of us to go. Are you interested?"

"Well how much are the tickets?"

"I think I'm getting them for free. I'll know for sure by Wednesday."

"Okay, count me in."

"Wonderful. I'm going to call the others."

Marlena hung up and Mercedes smiled. It would be fun to get together with just the ladies. It was getting kind of depressing being the only one of the four to not be in a relationship. Not that she wanted to be. She'd never had a boyfriend, never had sex, and didn't know why she was opposed to it. Maybe because she was used to being alone and making her own decisions? Perhaps she felt that a man, or men, would control her or ultimately have control over her? Or it could be the simple fact that she lost her parents when she was eighteen and had always taken care of herself and counted on herself and no one else. To actually let down her guard, or open her heart to another human being so deeply, scared the living daylights out of her.

It was easier to not make a connection or bond. Then it wouldn't hurt so badly when they disappointed her, or broke her heart, or left her.

It wasn't like she wasn't asked out. She got asked out a lot, but she wasn't interested. Funny thing was that she kind of liked Taylor, a deputy in the department. But that wouldn't be wise to get together with someone she worked with. It could only lead to disaster. Besides that, by the way things worked around here, brothers shared, and that meant a relationship with Kurt and Warner.

The thought made her nervous and afraid. Kurt and Warner traveled a lot. Both men had that whole bad boy, dark, mysterious look about them, and reputation. People avoided them. That couldn't be good. Plus they got together with the sheriff a lot on criminal matters she knew nothing about. When there was an intense situation like with Adele and her ex, she overhead Max talking with Warner over the phone and he did something, helped out somehow, and she wasn't supposed to know anything about it. Max saw her and warned her to not repeat what she heard and then stated that Warner had connections and was involved with the government years ago.

Sounded like trouble to her, and also like the kind of man that wasn't the commitment type, and neither was his brother Kurt. She heard through the town gossip that both men had dangerous professions, and no one really knew what they did. Some said they were spies, hit men, mercenaries, whatever. All she knew was it all sounded scary and she'd done scary all her life, she didn't need it now. Men like that would break her heart.

But God, the three of them were so good-looking, so intense and fierce they actually oozed masculinity, and made her body yearn to be touched. Maybe that was what really scared her? When Taylor, Kurt, and Warner had to watch over her when Marlena was in danger, she thought she was going to have a heart attack. The way Warner watched her with those deep, dark brown eyes, the hungry expression, and firm jaw, it was unnerving. He had a light beard on his chin and cheeks and his head was practically bald, his hair so short and military trimmed. His muscles? Oh God, he had muscles upon muscles and thinking of him holding her, pressing up against her, made her feel faint. Kurt and Taylor shared similar physiques, but Taylor's was always hidden beneath his uniform or a dress shirt. Kurt had dark black hair, deep blue eyes, and appeared to not have any hair on his chiseled chest. She took a deep breath and released it. Just thinking about them made her pussy clench. That couldn't be good. They would hurt her. Maybe not physically, but emotionally. They, like most military types, would expect too much. Their authority, mysterious professions put her on guard. She was tired of feeling on guard, and like everyone was out to get something from her. When she was struggling to make ends meet and take care of her parents, she had met a guy, Dexter. He seemed so sincere, had been a police officer in the neighborhood. He would check up on her and knew her family situation. He felt bad for her, well, more so, took advantage. It wasn't until he made a move and told her he could make all her sadness disappear.

At first she thought he cared for her, and actually wanted to help her, but then Dexter touched her, kissed her and told her that making love would ease the loneliness and they would have a good time. He was out for sex and nothing more. She learned fast that men couldn't be trusted. She also learned that a person's profession didn't define who they really were. Dexter was a cop, a man of authority, a peace-keeper, a symbol of honor and helpfulness. Yet he saw her, a young girl in high school losing her parents and being burdened by so much, that he tried taking advantage of that.

She knew there were bad people in every profession. Mercedes encountered plenty along the way. She didn't want to associate other officers in Chance with being manipulative or out for something, but she had that inkling of fear, that bit of resistance to accepting any man in uniform, of authority as being trustworthy. That's what kept her from acting on her feelings for Taylor. Yet she couldn't stop watching him, observing his character, his demeanor, and wondering if he could be trusted, and if he and his brothers were special.

She'd seen Taylor in action when he had an arrest. Just last week some drunk guy slammed his car into Billy Sue's car and sent the girl to the hospital. She had only been driving a year, but it wasn't her fault. Now the poor teenager feared driving. Taylor had been pissed off, especially since the guy was so drunk he tried to hit Taylor when he uncuffed him to fingerprint him into the system. In a flash Taylor slugged the guy, flipped him onto the floor on his belly, and cuffed him.

His agility, ability, swiftness, and strength both intimidated her and aroused her. But just like the flowers she saw in the store and didn't buy, she couldn't give in to carnal desires and lust. That instant see it, like it, buy into it way. It would only get her heart broken, make her feel like a loser again, and end in a disaster. She'd have to leave the sheriff's department, hell, leave Chance, because her reputation would be shot and everyone would think differently of her. No. She needed to stand her ground and look for the kind of man that fit into her life, her expectations. That was the safe route. That was the control she needed.

She swallowed hard and tried to convince herself that none of that attracted her to them. Then she thought about their ages. They were older. Much older. She knew better than to try and compare herself to an experienced woman. She wasn't.

What she needed was a guy her age. Maybe one who was soft-spoken, easy on the eyes of course, and not from Chance. She felt the spark of enthusiasm and then came the reality of it all. She never ventured out of town. With thoughts of how lame her life was, but safe, she loaded her car and headed home. She needed to get back to the station in thirty minutes.

* * * *

Kurt wondered why Mercedes hadn't bought the flowers. They were so beautiful, just like her. She hadn't gone for the red roses, the deep purple wildflowers but instead for the soft, feminine, arrangement of yellow flowers and tiny daisies. But that was Mercedes. She was sweet, kind, soft-spoken, and kind of shy, plus very ladylike. When he thought about the things that he assumed made her smile and made her happy, he thought about walks in the park, dinner and holding hands, candlelight and romance. She deserved it all. He never found it in himself to care about that stuff with a woman.

His relationships with the opposite sex were cut-and-dry. A few drinks, some small talk, and a sexual release that didn't leave him feeling guilty about leaving in the early morning hours or even right after the sex. Especially if it hadn't been good, or he realized he had been wearing beer goggles.

He shook the thoughts from his head. That was in the past. The last year had been difficult. He didn't want to be with anyone. He didn't want to get close or even get touched. He felt on edge, unworthy of connecting with a human being. Funny thing was, Warner was feeling the same way. But watching Mercedes, knowing that she didn't even notice him sneaking around watching her, made him feel protective. But the way she looked at those flowers, wanting them, had him making a move before he could reconsider and walk away.

"Hey, kid," he said to the store clerk stocking shelves by the floral section in the store.

"Yes, sir," he replied, not knowing who Kurt was. Teenagers were oblivious sometimes. No worries or real responsibilities. Those were the days.

"I need you to do me a favor," he said and then explained to the kid what he needed. He passed him a fifty-dollar bill and the kid was shocked and stared at it as if he never saw one before. Kurt had to chuckle inside. He gave him directions of what he needed and the kid agreed. Kurt also threatened him to not tell a soul. The kid took him seriously.

Smart kid.

Kurt headed out, paying for his things, and toward the direction of his black souped-up Camaro. He couldn't help but smile when he was in the privacy of his car and behind tinted windows. He felt good. He felt accomplished. Hopefully it would make Mercedes smile.

* * * *

Mercedes walked back into the sheriff's office after food shopping and grabbing a yogurt and granola bar for lunch. The first person she saw was Taylor and he looked pissed off. She looked away from him and noticed one of the other secretaries smiling wide.

"Looks like someone has an admirer," Thelma, the other secretary, said and Mercedes wondered what she meant as she took in the sight of a few other deputies.

"Who is he and when were you going to tell us?" Deputy Mike Spencer asked with his hand on his hip as he stood next to two other deputies.

"Tell you what, Mike?" she asked, walking by them slowly and unsure what the fuss was over. Then she spotted the large bouquet of yellow flowers on her desk.

She gasped.

"Oh my God," she said and hurried toward them. She touched the beautiful, delicate flowers and inhaled their scent. She felt so touched, so happy, and then she wondered who sent them. There was a card.

"Who sent them to you? Are you seeing someone?" Thelma asked, now up out of her chair and right beside Mercedes complimenting the bouquet.

"I'm not seeing anyone," she said and looked around her, immediately noticing Taylor.

"What does the card say?" he asked very seriously. She could tell that Mike was finding Taylor's reaction amusing. She didn't know why. Taylor was not pleasant to be around when he was pissed off.

She opened the envelope, pulled out the card, and read what it said, aloud.

"Just because you're as beautiful as these flowers. Hope they make you smile."

"Awe how sweet is that? My God, Mercedes, you don't have a clue as to who could have sent them?" Thelma asked.

"None," Mercedes said and then held the card against her chest as she leaned forward and smelled the flowers again.

"Whoever it was, they know what kind of flowers you like," Mike said to her.

"I saw these in the grocery store today when I did a little food shopping on my lunch break. Maybe someone saw me admiring them? But who?" Mercedes asked aloud.

"Sounds like a mystery, but I think everyone needs to get back to work. Taylor, can you head over toward the new construction site on the edge of town? Seems they're paving the roads and it's causing a lot of congestion and drivers are getting pissed off. Maybe some police presence will help people not lean down on the horn so much?" Sheriff Gordon said aloud, breaking up the crowd.

Mercedes looked at the flowers again and felt so happy inside. It was amazing what getting flowers could do to a woman.

"Mercedes, those are beautiful flowers. It's nice to see you smile so wide," Max told her then smiled at her before heading back to his office.

Mercedes couldn't help but feel bubbly inside. She put her password into her computer and began to get back to work. But she couldn't help but glance at the floral arrangement. She was touched and wished she knew who sent them so she could thank the person. Then she wondered why Taylor was so angry. Could he be jealous?

She shook her head at the thought. Why would Taylor care? He didn't like her in that way. And even if he did, she wouldn't get involved with a coworker. That was a big no-no. She pulled out her phone, took a picture of the flowers, and texted them to the girls. They were going to go crazy.

* * * *

"I thought you said that you forgot to take something out for dinner?" Taylor asked as he walked into the house after work. He was in such a pissed-off mood. He wondered who the fuck sent Mercedes those flowers. They were beautiful and he even went to the store to see if he could find out. When he asked the young clerk who had delivered the flowers, he told him the gentleman that bought them was very nice and not from town. He'd also given him fifty bucks.

"I picked up some food today and things."

Taylor went over to wash his hands.

"What's up with you?" Kurt asked him.

"Nothing."

"Bullshit, nothing. You look like you lost your best friend and want to go kill something. What gives?"

Taylor walked toward the counter and saw the food shopping bag and pushed it to the side to grab a handful of M&Ms that were in a bowl on the counter.

"Mercedes got a beautiful bouquet of flowers delivered to her today."

"What?" Kurt asked and then turned away.

"Yeah, really fucking nice ones. Some secret admirer or suave asshole. He fucking put a lame note on the card."

"What do you mean lame note?" Kurt asked, looking angry now, too. For a second there Taylor had thought his brother really didn't give a shit.

"The fucking card said something like, 'Just because you're as beautiful as these flowers. Hope they make you smile,' or some bullshit like that," Taylor told him.

Kurt looked like he was thinking about the words. "I don't know. That's kind of a nice compliment. They were beautiful flowers, right?" he asked.

Taylor stared at Kurt, who looked completely uncomfortable. Then he looked back at the counter.

"She said she saw them in the supermarket. I went there to find out who sent them but the kid said the guy gave him a fifty. You were at the store today. Was it you? Did you have those flowers delivered to her?"

Taylor saw Kurt trying to keep a straight face.

"Maybe."

"Holy shit!" Taylor ran his hands through his brown hair.

"Holy fucking shit. You have never done anything remotely romantic like that fucking ever, not even to get into Sally Anne's pants senior year of high school."

"Fuck you, I can be romantic if I fucking want to be," Kurt said then turned away and finished making dinner.

Taylor thought about it a moment. His brother did like Mercedes. He must like her a lot to do something like this.

"How did it happen? What made you do it?" Taylor couldn't help but to ask.

"You make it sound like I committed a crime and need penance. I fucking saw her in the supermarket staring at these gorgeous flowers. She looked at the price and then put them back down and walked away looking disappointed. I didn't think twice. I bought them, paid the clerk to deliver them and to keep his mouth shut, and that's the end of it. She was happy when she saw them? That was the point."

"Bro, she was beaming from ear to ear. I don't even think she cared about not knowing who sent them as much as she truly was touched by them. Me, on the other hand, was a fucking raging dick."

Kurt chuckled. "Oh man, what did you do?"

"Looked at her like she committed adultery. She's not even mine yet and I'm jealous of every guy who looks at her, asks her out, or flirts with her. This is insane."

"I heard from Warner an hour ago. He's coming home. He'll be here by Thursday."

"Thank God. We need to talk."

"I know we do. Let's wait for him. But you should rest a little easier knowing it was me who sent her those flowers and not some secret admirer."

Taylor smirked and nodded his head.

"It does."

"Good. So no more going around and threatening store clerks."

"I only slightly pushed him. Apparently you intimidated him more and you gave him fifty bucks."

"That's why I'm older and smarter than you."

"Screw you, you think you are. Wait until I tell Warner about your romantic side."

"Fuck you."

Taylor laughed and then headed toward the fridge for a bottle of water. He couldn't believe how relieved he felt, and even more importantly, optimistic, that Mercedes would one day belong to him and his brothers and they would treat her as special as she deserved to be treated. He just needed to be patient.

Chapter 2

Mercedes, Marlena, Alicia, and Adele were laughing as they headed out of the comedy show. Wager County was a beautiful area right outside of Chance. It was built up with lots of storefronts, a movie theatre, a small shopping mall, and a few big chain superstores. There was a really famous bar and restaurant called Bobby's Treasure Chest. They offered fresh seafood, a raw bar, restaurant, and connected to it was a dance club. It had an upscale bar with an outdoor deck and bar that overlooked the water.

"Danny and Jack made us reservations at Bobby's Treasure Chest. Their friends own the place," Marlena told them as they headed across the street and down the block.

"God, it's such a warm night. I don't even need this sweater," Alicia said as she took off the light sweater and placed it over her purse, tying the arms of it to the strap.

"Well it was a bit chilly in the comedy club. But out here is beautiful," Adele added and she hugged Mercedes's arm as they all walked down the street together.

"Oh my, look at that place," Marlena said and pointed at the storefront of a lingerie store. There was a sexy red negligee hanging in the window along with some other upscale items.

"Let's check it out. Maybe I'll bring the Ferguson brothers a little surprise home," Adele said and let go of Mercedes's arm to open the door.

"You guys go inside, I'll wait here," Mercedes said, feeling uncomfortable.

Marlena grabbed her arm and pulled her along with them.

"No, you won't. You're coming in, too," Marlena told her and led her into the store.

Everyone walked around the place and Mercedes had to admit that the woman had gorgeous stuff.

"Can I help you find anything specific?" a woman asked and when Mercedes turned around she recognized Jessica. She lived in Chance with her mom and dad. She was three years younger than Mercedes.

"Hi, Jessica, how are you? I didn't know you worked here?" Mercedes asked as Jessica hugged her hello.

"My mom owns the place and now I work here, too. With my background in fashion and design I get to help my mom keep up with the latest fashions and styles."

"Well you have beautiful things," Mercedes said as she admired some panties and matching bras.

"Are you shopping for yourself, or looking to please your boyfriend?"

Mercedes felt her cheeks warm.

"No boyfriend, and my friends are doing the shopping. They're all involved in relationships."

"Nice. And they drag you in here to look at sexy lingerie," Jessica said, teasing her.

"Great friends, right?"

"We are great friends," Marlena said and then pressed a set of matching panties and bra to Mercedes's chest.

"These would look fabulous on you, and even if no one but you gets to see them, they'll make you feel sexy and beautiful just like you are," Marlena told her and smiled.

"That is true. There's something about a sexy pair of panties and bra that just make a woman feel incredible and alive," Jessica added.

Mercedes introduced Jessica to the girls and they all said hello as they carried their items to the register.

Mercedes looked at the prices on the bra and panties then felt the hand on her shoulder.

"They're on me. But you have to promise to tell me when you find out who your secret admirer is," Marlena said, taking the set from Mercedes's hands and passing them to Jessica. Mercedes tried to talk her out of buying the set for her but her friends and Jessica countered her arguments and a few minutes later the four of them all walked out with pretty purple bags containing items from J.J.'s Lingerie.

As they got to the restaurant, the hostess told them that they needed to wait about fifteen minutes. They headed toward the bar to get a drink and wait. As Mercedes sipped at her glass of white wine, she looked around at the establishment. It was decorated like a fisherman's ship with old-fashioned fishing tools, some netting, and artificial crabs and lobsters on the walls. It was a fun and lively atmosphere as the sound of live music playing at the connected club next door filtered into the main bar area and restaurant. Jimmy Buffett's "Margaritaville" was playing, and Mercedes and Adel were laughing because they'd ordered margaritas to drink.

As she glanced around the place, her eyes caught sight of two men sitting at a high bar table in the corner. One of the guys' eyes locked on her as the guy next to him continued to speak. He looked her over. She saw the way his eyes slowly roamed her body from across the way and then he smiled.

She felt embarrassed and shy as she looked away and then focused on her friends talking. She couldn't help but to glance back toward the man and now both men looked at her. The other one smiled softly and she looked away. Two guys? Two strange men both looking at her at the same time? She felt uneasy, unfamiliar with what she should do.

"Hey, are you okay?" Adele asked her. Mercedes looked past Adele's shoulder and saw the guys still watching and talking to one another. Adele looked that way and then back at Mercedes.

"Oh my God, they're hot."

"Are they?" Mercedes asked and took a sip from her drink.

"Don't even try to deny that you're checking them out."

"Checking who out?" Marlena asked, and Adele told her, and she looked, and then Alicia looked.

"Oh God don't look at them or they'll come over here."

"And what's wrong with that?" Adele asked.

"They might try to flirt or ask me out or something."

Adele looked back over that way.

"I think or something, by the looks of those two."

Mercedes gasped and felt her cheeks turned red.

"Stop that, Adele, you're scaring her," Alicia scolded Adele and Adele got serious.

"Sorry. But hey, if they do flirt with you, go for it. You have turned down so many offers in Chance, not wanting to get together with someone from town that you know, in fear that if it goes wrong you'll be embarrassed."

"Yeah, so this could be a good opportunity," Alicia added.

"Or maybe not. Maybe she just needs to stick to three certain men in Chance that can't keep their eyes off of her either," Marlena said and smirked then took a sip from her margarita.

"Who?" Mercedes asked.

"Oh you know who. The Dawn men," Adele told her.

"Not happening. They scare me. They're not the commitment types. They have dangerous jobs that take two of them out of town for months at a time, and they're too experienced and older than I am," she told them.

They started talking through her concerns and everyone but Marlena seemed convinced that maybe the Dawn men weren't the commitment types and were too hard and intense to trust. She appreciated their feedback and talking through her fears, but she also felt a little guilty. It was strange.

"Your table is ready, ladies," the hostess said as she interrupted their conversation. Mercedes couldn't help but to glance where the two men sat and as she walked by they continued to watch her. She gave a soft smile and both of them smiled wide. That wasn't so hard, she thought as she headed into the other room.

* * * *

"It's good to have you back, bro. We missed you," Taylor told Warner as they sat at one of the private booths along with Jack, Danny, and Mike Spencer at Spencer's.

"It sure is good to be back," Warner said as he eased into the seat.

"So have you guys thought much about our proposition with security yet, or is a day too little time?" Jack asked and smirked.

Taylor and Kurt looked at Warner.

"We're discussing the opportunity still. I don't know if Max has mentioned this or not, but your security team should really be up to speed with some of the crazy shit going on in clubs nearby," Warner told them.

"Like what?" Mike asked.

"Like the shady characters coming in and trying to sell drugs, prostitution, and even abducting women," Warner said.

"You mean like sex slave business stuff?" Danny asked, sitting forward and looking sick.

"Not quite and not on that scale. There's this new thing where guys come in on a regular basis and scope out a place. They see who the regulars are and the types of women that frequent the place. You know people stick to the same routine a lot and that's when they become victims. So anyway, these guys take pictures of them or just right there on the spot text to a group of men looking for a certain type of woman. They give a description a cost and then they get paid and the guys get the location. They come in, snag the woman in some suave way, or they pay extra to have someone else do it, and the woman leaves with the man or makes plans to meet and boom, she's taken," Warner explained.

"That's fucking sick," Danny said.

"What happens to the women? Are they killed?" Jack asked, seemingly just as angry and sick as Danny about the information. Warner looked at Mike.

"Some wind up dead, others wind up in the hospital, not even remembering what happened because they were drugged, and of course others that do remember are embarrassed so they don't do anything. It's crazy," Mike said and then took a slug of beer and looked around the place.

"Well we don't want anything like that happening here. What do we have our security look for? How can we be diligent to stop anything like that from happening here?" Jack asked.

"It's hard, but having the right security team and the same men and women looking around and recognizing the regulars can help. It's believed that these types of individuals don't hit the smaller places. Their faces become too obvious and recognizable. It's small time so they do a lot of changing of people, these spotters, if you want to call them that," Warner told them.

"I think I can speak for my brothers and Marlena by saying we want to have the best security in the business. When the new addition is finally open in a few weeks, we want precautions in place, and most importantly our patrons to be safe. So any advice would be appreciated but of course your involvement and working hand in hand with us would be even better," Danny said and raised his beer up to toast them. They clinked beers and laughed then Mike glanced at his cell phone."

"You okay?" Kurt asked him.

"Yeah, why?"

"You keep checking your cell phone. Waiting on a call or text?" Kurt pushed and Mike smirked.

"Waiting to hear from Marlena," he replied.

"Oh, she's not at home?" Taylor asked then took a slug of beer.

"No, she and the girls went out tonight," Jack said.

Warner wondered if Mercedes were with them. He glanced at his brothers. Since he arrived home Thursday that was all Taylor kept pushing. A conversation about making a serious move on Mercedes and getting to know her. Warner had done a lot of thinking while he was on this last job. He hadn't even told his brothers about the near death experience. It would only make Taylor angrier at him. He hid the bandage on his arm well. It was just a scratch from the bullet. A bullet that never should have gotten that close to hitting him. An indication that maybe he was losing his focus and his edge.

"Where did they go?" Taylor asked.

"It was the four of them? The crew?" Kurt teased, but it was his way of asking if Mercedes went without coming straight out and asking.

Mike chuckled.

"Mercedes is with them, if that's what you want to know."

"I didn't say that." Kurt stated.

"But you want to know?" Danny added.

"When are you guys going to make a move? I mean what the fuck are you waiting for? The woman got flowers from a secret admirer today," Mike said to them, sounding angry. Warner didn't react. He knew damn well that his brother sent them to her. What a shock that had been, and it led to some ribbing earlier and a few fists being thrown.

"I'm not worried about that," Taylor said with confidence.

"You're not? What changed from that look of death you were giving Mercedes and the attitude you had with everyone else?" Mike asked.

"I was fine. I'm not worried."

Mike's phone rang.

"It's Marlena."

He said a few words. He smiled and then he glanced at Warner, Taylor, and Kurt. "I see. Well tell her to be careful. Make plans for a local place, maybe here in Chance. Okay then in Wager County.

Someplace busy. All right I can give her the riot act before the date. When will you be back? Okay. Love ya, too." Mike disconnected the call.

"How sweet," Taylor teased him.

"Don't be messing with me. You guys have your own worries, Mr. Confident," Mike told them.

"Worries? Why is that?" Taylor asked.

Mike looked at the three Dawn brothers and then at Warner.

"Seems Mercedes met these two guys at Bobby's Treasure Chest after the comedy show. Marlena said she's talking to them right now and making plans for a date."

Warner felt jealousy and anger hit his gut. They fucking waited too long. He never should have gone on this last mission. What the fuck was he thinking?

"Well, she's a very attractive, sweet young woman. You snooze, you lose," Danny teased.

"Maybe it will be a disaster of a date?" Taylor said.

"Maybe we should find out who these guys are and make sure that they're good enough for her," Kurt suggested and then made a face as if his own words made him sick. He rolled his tongue over his teeth then took a slug of beer, turning away.

"Maybe she'll go on this date and won't like them. She doesn't know these men and they apparently aren't from Chance, which means we do kind of have the authority, inconspicuously, I might add, to ensure she is safe on this date," Mike said to them and raised both of his eyebrows as if saying they knew what he meant.

"Well then, you three have a job to do tonight," Taylor told them.

"What's that?" Mike asked.

"The time, the place, and the location of this date. Need I say more," Kurt said very seriously. Mike just shook his head. Even their good friends knew when Kurt and his brothers were pissed off and when not to tease. But Warner felt sick and angry. He wanted to call it a night and make a plan. He needed to keep calm and pretend this wasn't as big of a deal as it felt. Mercedes could get swept off her feet by two men. Two guys who would try to touch her, kiss her, maybe even fuck her. He squeezed the beer bottle so tight then felt his arm ache and slowly released it. He needed to be calm. Mercedes would be their woman. They couldn't have lost the opportunity because he was being a stubborn dick. They just couldn't.

* * * *

Mercedes couldn't help the uneasy feeling she had talking to the two men. One of them seemed more interested than the other one and that guy tended to just say things to add to the conversation. But the one really flirting was very attractive and close to her age. In her mind she thought he seemed perfect in her notebook description of the right type of guy for her. He had a normal job, something in business and finance. He lived nearby, he said near the beach so he must make descent money, and he was very polite and a complete gentleman. In fact when he asked for her number and she seemed hesitant to give it to a stranger she'd just met, he offered her a business card and his name and cell number, office number, even fax number. He seemed genuinely kind.

"So, if you feel more comfortable meeting us someplace locally, how about here, tomorrow night? Maybe around seven?" he asked as he held her gaze. He had blonde hair and the cutest dimple in his left cheek. He seemed preppy and conservative. He wore a blue Ralph Lauren polo shirt and his friend wore a Dior one in navy blue. He had a bit more olive complexion and his hair was darker, like Kurt's. As she thought the thought she felt guilty again. Now she was comparing two guys she'd just met, and was making plans to meet again, with Kurt and his brothers. When would she get them out of her head and stop comparing every guy she met to them?

"Okay, we can meet here tomorrow night at seven. I'd better get back to my friends. I've already made them stay too long."

"We could give you a ride home," he suggested and smiled softly.

She shook her head. "I don't know you, remember."

"Well, we're going to take care of that tomorrow night. I was just being helpful, not trying anything," he said to her and his tone was a little odd, but she figured it was just her. She wasn't used to dating. She never said yes, until now, and probably because she was trying to get the Dawn brothers out of her head.

"Bye," she said and they shook hands even though he leaned a little closer and lower as if he may kiss her cheek good-bye.

She headed toward her friends and the questions began as they made their way out of the club.

"They are very good-looking. So when is the date?" Adel asked her, and she told them all the details and they talked about what she should wear.

"Maybe even the new panties and bra set you just purchased," Alicia teased and winked.

"No way. I'm not that kind of girl," she replied and they smiled and told her they were kidding and then talked to her about being careful and she loved them for it.

Chapter 3

Mercedes was a nervous wreck as she drove her little beat-up Jetta to Wager County. She had mixed emotions about this date. Initially it was just the typical expectations of first dates, getting to know Jeff and Damien and how this could turn out. Like what if she liked them and they didn't like her or if one of them liked her and the other didn't. Then her mind traveled to Kurt, Taylor, and Warner. She felt sick, guilty, and of course began to compare all five of the men.

She almost cancelled as she thought about her feelings for Taylor, Warner, and Kurt and how she was truly avoiding them out of her own fears. Maybe Jeff and Damien would be better for her and more compatible. Hell, maybe just Jeff would be and she would be fine with that. As she parked her car she hoped that they were nice and that they didn't try to kiss her. The thought gave her more guilt and she had to yell at herself for being stupid. Kurt, Warner, and Taylor were too old for her, too experienced, and too unreliable. Plus they didn't like her like that. If they liked her it was probably just for sex because the attraction was there. She didn't need that. This date was an opportunity to get more experience and see what types of men were out there. Nothing more would come of it unless it went really well and they asked her out again. But first she needed to get through this first date and her nerves. God, she was so inexperienced, she probably looked like a clueless virgin at age twenty-six. Damn it.

She got out of her car, locked the door, and then placed her keys in her bag. She smoothed out the pale green dress she wore that hit right above the knees, only showing off some thigh skin, but the matching heels made her legs look sexy. The dress had spaghetti straps and was cut right across where her cleavage began. Not too low, conservative, sort of considering she was well endowed and it was difficult to find nice dresses that didn't show off too much.

She walked through the open doorway and was greeted by the hostess but before she could explain that she was meeting someone, Jeff appeared. He was alone and she felt her heart sink a little. The feelings of not being good enough for Damien hit her at once. That was her own lack of self-confidence but she smiled wide and shook his hand hello. Jeff stepped closer and kissed her cheek then stepped back, still holding her hand and looked her over. "You look so beautiful and so sweet. Like an angel," he said and winked. She supposed that was a good description of her character. She was conservative, soft spoken, and sort of shy. Suddenly she wondered if she should have worn the low-cut, black, slim-fitting dress that Adele had suggested. Then Jeff would be drooling over her.

He led her inside to a table where she saw Damien sitting and talking on a cell phone. He held it in front of him and it seemed like he took a picture or two of her as she approached. A compliment or kind of creepy? She wasn't sure. He put the phone down and stood up, kissed her cheek hello, looked her over as if appraising her dress and seeing if it were designer or not. He definitely had expectations in his women. She could dress designer but not on her salary. She felt a little strange.

She sat down and they had already ordered a bottle of wine. Jeff poured her a glass.

"I have to admit, it was torture not seeing you for so many hours," Jeff said and then clinked his wine glass to hers. Damien did the same and held her gaze.

"That's very sweet of you," she replied.

"You are the sweet one, Mercedes," Damien said and took another sip of his wine.

"So, you live in the town after Wager, how are the restaurants and bars there?" Jeff asked her and she told him about Spencer's.

"I have to be honest, I've never been there before. Our work tends to bring us to more exotic places like the Caribbean, Puerto Rico, and even Hawaii. How about you? Travel a lot?"

"No, I'm a secretary for a business in Chance. I work a lot of hours," she said and didn't want to tell them that it was the sheriff's department. Some guys were intimidated by that. They might feel like she could get them into trouble if they overstepped their bounds or hurt her feelings. She probably could if she wanted to but that wasn't her. She just wanted to be liked for who she was and not for anything else.

They looked over the menus, ordered, and then talked some more. Jeff took many opportunities to touch her skin, to caress her hair, and even stare into her eyes.

"Your eyes are hazel, not brown. Very nice," Jeff said and smiled softly.

"I thought they were brown, but they do look so stunning and stand out, especially with your hair. It's brown with red highlights. I like it," Damien said and then she saw him with his phone again. Jeff pressed his fingers to her chin, turning her face toward him. She had a funny feeling. The more she talked to these men it seemed like they were sizing her up as much as she was sizing them up. Damien looked at his phone a lot and Jeff occupied most of the conversation, but the little comments Damien added still made her think he found her attractive. She was so confused and clueless about men and dating. She needed to really pay attention and learn, but she wanted to see if there was an attraction. They seemed to be shopping.

"Our business tends to keep us very busy and we get interrupted often, but don't worry, that's why there are two of us," Jeff said and touched his finger to her lip, pulled back, and smiled.

She felt intimidated to say the least as she glanced at Damien.

"Does that interest you, or are you shy, having two men wanting to pay attention to you, date you?" he asked.

She swallowed hard.

"I never considered it before," she replied. A total lie. She considered three men. Warner, Taylor, and Kurt. What was she doing here?

"Really, you've never been involved with multiple men at once?" he asked and brought her hand to his lips and kissed the top. She shook her head. He smiled, glanced at Damien, and then lowered her hand.

"The food is here." She clasped her hands together as she saw the lobster tails. She hadn't wanted him to order something so costly but he insisted that she would love them, and he and Damien were in the mood for them.

"Perfect. Let's enjoy our meal and then maybe go to the bar for a drink or perhaps a walk out by the marina. It's a lovely night," he said and she smiled then went about eating. They talked some more and Jeff made her laugh a few times. He was funny, and seemed very nice, but she wasn't really attracted to him. But she hadn't been out on a date in forever so she enjoyed their company.

* * * *

"He picks up her hand and fucking kisses it one more time and I'm going to lose my fucking mind," Kurt said to Taylor.

"Join the fucking club," Taylor said into his wrist mic. Warner had stayed home. He was sick and felt that he'd make them lose their opportunity with Mercedes. They all knew how gorgeous she was and kind, and any man who grabbed her attention would be in heaven to have her. They should have made a move. Now they were watching over her and this first date with two dickheads they knew nothing about. But they took a lot of pictures. If these guys broke her heart, they would make their lives a living hell.

* * * *

Mercedes walked along the boardwalk by the marina with Jeff on one side and Damien on the other. They ran out of things to talk about and she turned toward them as they stopped by the end and near a set of stairs that led back up to the parking lot at the side of the building. It was darker down here, and only two low-lit lampposts lit the area.

"Well, I think I should call it a night. I have to drive back and I have a lot to do tomorrow," she said and Damien squinted his eyes at her but Jeff pulled her closer. He cupped her cheek and looked down into her eyes.

"Do you have to? The night is young," he said and as she went to answer him, he kissed her.

She knew instantly that she didn't have those feelings for him. She pressed her hands against his chest and pulled back. She took a retreating step.

"I'm sorry, Jeff. I think I should go."

"Are you sure?" Damien asked her and she nodded her head and headed up the stairs. She got to the top of the stairs and Jeff stopped her.

Damien wasn't in sight.

"I'm sorry if I came on too strong. You looked so pretty in the moonlight and I truly enjoyed our conversation this evening. I hoped that you would consider getting to know us better," he said and caressed her skin.

"Your skin is so soft and you smell so good. You're exactly what they had in mind."

"They?" she asked as he walked with her and held her hand. She heard the screeching sound of tires and then felt him lift her up and hurry toward a dark Navigator. The door swung open. She was scared and instantly began to fight. She didn't know what the hell was happening and she kicked him hard. He dropped her to the ground and then went for her and she punched him in the eye. He swung at her.

"Stupid bitch," he yelled and swung again, hitting her jaw, her cheek, and then he ripped her dress as he pulled her up by the top.

"Stop right there. Stop!" a deep voice yelled. Jeff shoved her, jumped into the Navigator, and sped out of the parking lot.

"Mercedes. Baby, are you okay?" Kurt asked her and she could hear Taylor yelling into his phone and giving a description of the vehicle and asking for police to respond to an attempted abduction.

She was crying. The pain and the fear of what happened set in and Kurt pulled her into his arms and held her tight. She cried against his shoulder, the feel of his body—hard, comforting, protective—easing her hysterical state.

She slowly pulled back and Taylor bent down on his knee and softly pushed her hair from her face. She looked at both of them.

"Son of a bitch. I'm going to find those fucking assholes and kill them," Kurt said and she shook in his arms.

"You're scaring her, bro. Ease up. She's safe. Thank God we were here," Taylor said and used his thumb to brush away the tears from her eyes.

"I don't know what happened. Why were you here?" she asked them.

"We were watching over you, Mercedes. Things are going to change. This shit is never going to happen again," Kurt told her. Dark blue eyes held hers and then he placed his hand against the back of her head and pressed her face back to his chest and held her tight. She couldn't stop shaking. Jeff and Damien tried to abduct her. What were they planning on doing to her? Crazy thoughts went through her head as sirens blared in the distance. Then it hit her. Taylor and Kurt had been there watching her. They'd known she was on a date. They seemed angry, but they saved her life. Did they have deeper feelings for her than what they revealed? Where was Warner? Maybe he didn't care. This was a mess. *I could have gotten taken, raped and even killed tonight. How stupid of me to think they were nice guys. Oh God, how embarrassing. Kurt and Taylor will think I'm naive and stupid, immature and a child.*

She pulled back.

"Let me up. I'm fine," she said and he looked at her strangely then helped her to stand on shaky legs. The police were there immediately and they looked angry as they looked her over. Kurt pulled up the material of her dress that lowered so much that her cleavage was showing. Someone handed Taylor a police windbreaker and Taylor handed it to Kurt who helped to cover her.

"They lost sight of the Navigator. We have patrols out looking," the officer said.

"Fuck," Taylor yelled, and she jumped and Kurt pulled her close to him and wrapped his arm around her waist, holding her by his side.

"But we have the full license plate and a description of these guys. They won't get away with this. We'll find them," the officer said and Taylor mumbled something incoherent.

"Miss, can you come with me? I have some questions for you and we need to document those injuries," the officer said.

She went to move.

"We'll bring her over. She's with us. We'll get her home to Chance," Kurt said and she didn't say a word. She knew better than to argue with men from Chance and especially Kurt and Taylor. They would get her home safely, and then it would all sink in and she would be scared to go anywhere. *I was attacked and nearly abducted by two men I had dinner with? This is so embarrassing.*

* * * *

"I want to know who the fuck these men are and how the hell they disappeared and no one can find their vehicle or their whereabouts." Warner yelled into his cell phone. He was standing outside of Mercedes's home along with his brothers, Mike, and the sheriff. Dr. Anders was inside with Mercedes and all her friends were there with their men, too. It was a fucking madhouse.

But Kurt was still on edge and angry at what took place. If they hadn't been there, watching over Mercedes, then those men would have abducted her. They'd meant her harm. They'd hit her like it was nothing and the sight of those bruises enraged him. If only he had gotten to her sooner, he could have at least grabbed the guy who assaulted her. But he and Taylor were calling it an end to the night when they saw the guy kiss Mercedes. Their hearts were heavy and as they headed out to the parking lot they heard the squealing of tires, saw Mercedes fighting off the guy who held her over the shoulder, and then him hitting her. He would never get the images out of his head. Never.

Kurt paced and Taylor was talking to Mike, Will, Leo, and Hank.

"Well work on it. I want full involvement and if you don't have the fucking answers I want by nine a.m. then I'm taking full control and calling in my people," Warner said and disconnected the call. He placed his hands on his hips and explained what the police and detectives in Wager County had thus far along with the state police.

"They don't seem like they're on top of this or taking it too seriously," Max said, looking upset.

"They aren't. They almost sound like they fucking think it was just two guys trying to take advantage of a young woman on a date. They tried to tell me that no other similar situations have occurred in Wager or any nearby locations. I just think they don't have the man power or the resources to really investigate this properly. It's not their fault, but I'm not leaving this up to them. I'm going to get involved. We're going to," Warner said and looked at Kurt. Kurt nodded his head.

"I am, too. She's our responsibility," Taylor stated and he was straight-faced and firm.

"So you're making an official claim to Mercedes? As protectors?" Max added as he asked them and held Warner's gaze.

"She's ours. This never should have happened and nothing like this will ever happen to her again. That good enough for you, Max?" Warner asked but didn't wait for a reply. He looked at Kurt.

"Let Taylor remain here for the night with her. You and I have some investigating to do and some calls to make. I want those assholes behind bars within twenty-four hours. They're already hours ahead of us. You know what we need to do," he said and Kurt nodded his head.

"Take care of her, Taylor, and we'll touch base later," Kurt told Taylor and Taylor nodded.

Kurt glanced toward the house and worried about Mercedes's safety. But she would have lots of people around her for the next week at least. Plus Taylor was there. He'd stay right in her room with his gun cocked and ready if necessary just for peace of mind.

He caught up to Warner and got into the truck.

Warner stepped on the gas and got out of there.

"Call Breaker, have him notify Slick, Pinto, and Gemini that we need their skills."

"Seriously?" Kurt asked as he pulled out his cell phone. Warner looked at him.

"You guys went over your part of the story of what happened tonight and Mercedes went over hers. This was not some slick game two assholes wanted to play out with some innocent unknowing female. It has all the indicators of something bigger," Warner told him as he stepped on the gas and headed home.

Taylor didn't like the sound of that and he instantly knew where his brother was heading. He thought about the conversation at Spencer's with Mike, Danny, and Jack.

"You think this could be part of one of those groups you mentioned at Spencer's?"

Warner didn't even look his way.

"Think about what we know thus far. Think about the extent these individuals went to grab Mercedes."

Kurt felt his blood pressure boiling.

"I'm with you on this. I'll do whatever is necessary to find these guys before they try to hurt another woman."

Warner nodded his head and Kurt took an unsteady breath. They could have lost Mercedes tonight. Those men could have done terrible things to her or even sold her for money. Bile rose in his throat and he tried swallowing it down as Warner pulled onto the long private road then to their home. They would find the men responsible. They would protect Mercedes from here on out and prove to her that she belonged with them and was safe with them forever.

Chapter 4

Mercedes cried out, striking against the solid chest and feeling the heat of a solid heavy body next to her.

"Mercedes, it's me. It's Taylor, baby. You're safe," Taylor said. His voice penetrated her dreams and she blinked her eyes open, feeling the tears leak from her eyes.

She was breathing heavily and her cheek and jaw hurt. She scrunched her eyes together and gulped hard.

"Easy now. Your cheek and jaw are bruised up and your shoulder and chest, too," he told her as she leaned back down, placing her head against the pillow. She was wearing a T-shirt, no bra, and a pair of light cotton shorts. Taylor had no shirt on but wore jeans. She tried not to look at all his muscles and the ridges of abdominal muscles from under his pecs to the waist of his jeans. He was mega fit and she felt her cheeks warm and turned away.

He reached over and caressed her damp locks away from her cheeks. He smiled softly.

"You're safe. I'm not leaving you," he whispered to her.

She moved, feeling overheated, completely aroused, and also a bit scared. He was a big man, a muscular man, and a deputy who worked where she worked. He shouldn't be on her bed, almost naked.

"You shouldn't be on my bed with me. It's not appropriate," she said to him, feeling the anxiety of her words.

Taylor smiled softly and caressed her chin.

"I'm protecting you. I saw what went down tonight, remember? I need to be close to you and I want you to feel safe. What you went through was traumatic." He caressed her chin and gave her a wink. Her core tightened and her pussy clenched. She was such a loser.

"Did Marlena and the others go home?" she asked, feeling nervous at the way Taylor stared at her and caressed her hair.

"A couple of hours ago," he replied and continued to stroke her hair.

"Did they find Jeff and Damien?" she asked and his fingers stopped moving in her hair. She cringed as his expression changed. He pulled back and appeared as if he were biting the inside of his cheek.

"Not yet, but don't worry, we'll find them."

She felt the tears fill her eyes as she thought about the fact the two men were still out there and that they wanted to hurt her.

"Awe, baby, please stop crying. You're safe now. My brothers and I will make sure of it." He leaned closer and he kissed her forehead as he leaned one arm over her waist and used his other hand to wipe away the tears.

"I feel so stupid," she said and snorted. "You should go. I appreciate your kindness and the fact that you feel you need to stay here after helping to save me, but it's not necessary. I'll be just fine."

He shook his head.

"Baby, you never should have been in that position to begin with," he said to her in that tone that was all Taylor's.

"I know that. I was stupid, and naïve to have accepted a date with two men I didn't know. But they seemed so nice and I don't date and then my friends were like go for it, and well I got caught up in it all and I forgot everything I learned living on the—" She stopped talking. She almost said that she lived on the streets. What would Taylor think of her? God, how stupid. She couldn't think. Not with him this close to her and his damn sexy body leaning against hers.

"On the what? What were you going to say?"

"Nothing. Nothing at all. I'm rambling. I'm okay. I need to get up," she said and he looked reluctant to get up from the bed. But he did and stared at her. She pulled back the covers and his eyes roamed over her thighs and the short shorts she wore. Adele had grabbed what she could find and helped her earlier. Why had she chosen such a sexy pair of pajamas for her to wear to bed knowing that Taylor was staying here to watch over her? She wondered if Adele was playing matchmaker.

"Let me help you," Taylor said, standing up at his full height of six foot three and she gulped. He was huge. Looked extra large in her small bedroom. She reached out and took his hand and he pulled her up slowly, letting his other hand wrap around her waist and she felt his fingers over part of her ass and lower back. He was just so big.

"Ouch," she said and placed her hand over her waist by her hip bone. Taylor scrunched his eyes together and held her by her shoulders as he bent slightly.

"You're hurt there, too?" he asked and she nodded her head then reached for the hem of her T-shirt to lift it slightly. Taylor knelt down on one knee and kept a hand on her left side over her hip as she lifted her shirt and he looked at her skin.

"Jesus. You're all bruised up. You didn't show Dr. Anders this last night?" he asked and she shook her head.

"It didn't hurt last night. My cheek and jaw hurt the most and of course my shoulder," She said.

He looked up at her and held her gaze.

"You never should have been there last night," He said and she felt like shit. He was reprimanding her and basically calling her stupid.

Before she could respond his cell phone rang.

"I'll wait here," he told her, but it seemed like that wasn't what he wanted to say.

She turned around and headed into the bathroom.

* * * *

"How is Mercedes?" Kurt asked as Taylor answered the phone. He and Warner had been up all night. The team was working overtime to get info on these guys.

"Yes, she just woke up. She's sore and has more bruising on her hip."

"How do you know that?" Kurt asked.

"She was achy and then I checked out the area under her shirt. She's bruised up good. Plus she blames herself. She's been crying, and she told me to leave."

* * * *

"You make her understand that things are going to change."

"It would be better if you two were here, too, when I explain. That way she gets it," Taylor told Kurt.

"Warner isn't exactly pleasant and neither am I. Make sure you stay with her. We'll try to stop by soon," Kurt said and then disconnected the call.

Kurt's eyes burned as he rubbed them and felt the throbbing headache.

He exhaled, reached for the painkillers and the bottle of water. He took two and swallowed, hoping they would kick in fast.

"Is she okay?" Warner asked.

"She's in pain and feeling responsible for what happened."

Warner scrunched his eyebrows together. "She can blame me. If I wasn't such a dick and didn't leave for that fucking trip then she wouldn't have been in that situation. She'd be in our bed by now, protected from dicks like these two fuckheads."

"You can't say that. It wasn't what was meant to be. You weren't ready and I was still working my own fears and hesitation out. Plus you completed your mission, came back safely, and we're here now. We'll protect her."

Warner leaned back in the chair and stretched his arms out above his head.

"What's that?" Kurt asked and Warner didn't move. He held his brother's gaze and Kurt sat forward.

"That last job was different than the others."

Kurt didn't like the way that sounded.

"Different how?" Kurt asked.

Warner held his gaze.

"Nothing to worry about, I wasn't a hundred percent on my game. But I made it. I'm here now, and things are going to be different. I'm not taking those kinds of chances anymore. I'm not."

"So you're not going to tell me anything more about it?" Kurt asked.

"Have we ever asked one another questions about what we do and where we went and what went down? No, so we're not going to now."

Kurt took a deep breath. He really wished the painkillers would kick in. Now he felt even worse than before.

"Well, I'm glad you made it back, in one piece."

Warner nodded his head. "We could have lost Mercedes, you realize that right?" he asked Kurt and Kurt immediately nodded.

"That's what gets me so pissed off and fired up the most, the fact that my stubbornness, denial, fear of letting down my guard and opening my heart to such a sweet woman could have been lost. These men, the things they do to these women."

"I know. I know, Warner, and I try not to think about it because it makes me sick, it scares the fuck out of me, and I know the bottom line is that she's safe. That Taylor and I were there and we got to her in time. We need to make this up to her. We need to be honest with her. Together."

Warner let down his arms and nodded his head.

"Shower first then we'll bring over food. Let Taylor know to give us thirty minutes."

Kurt nodded his head as Warner left the room. He texted Taylor then stood up. His brother could have died. Their woman could have been raped, sold to some high bidder, or even killed. It was time to take a chance and open up their hearts. This was a second chance and one he was going to make sure him and his brothers didn't miss out on.

* * * *

Mercedes entered the bedroom after taking a quick shower. The window was open, a soft breeze filled the room, and it seemed so quiet. Too quiet. She stopped where she was. Listened for any sounds, any indication that Taylor was still there in her home, but she heard nothing. Tears filled her eyes but didn't fall. Well she told him to leave, so maybe he listened. He was just a friend, a coworker. Yeah right. *Keep lying to yourself, Mercedes. He was more than that. You feel it, too.*

What she hadn't expected was the fear that began to form in her belly. The quietness scared her. Being alone suddenly scared her and when she heard the floor creak outside her door she gasped and covered her mouth.

She was shaking and she couldn't stop herself.

The door began to push open and she heard Taylor's voice.

"Mercedes, are you finished? Is it okay for me to come in?"

"Oh God," she said and covered her face with her hands. A moment later she felt his strong arms wrap around her and she hugged him tight. She held on to him, breathed in his scent, his cologne and the feel of the T-shirt he wore pressed against her cheek. She was disappointed that he wasn't bare chested. The thought was instant. He rubbed her back and her hair.

"You're okay. You're safe. We didn't leave you," he said to her. The floor creaked again as his words sunk in. They didn't leave her.

She pulled back slightly and saw Kurt standing there. Kurt, six foot three, dark black hair, blue eyes, and he wore a light blue shirt with blue jeans that made those sexy eyes stand out even more. He looked incredible.

He stepped closer as Taylor released her slowly.

"It's all right to be scared. That will take some time to get rid of," Kurt said as he reached out and cupped her good cheek. Taylor moved out of the way and Kurt placed a hand on her waist. He used his thumb to caress her lip.

"Some ice will bring the swelling down, but first, we brought over some food," he said. She nodded her head and he held her gaze.

Kurt just stared at her and she wondered what he would do. She looked at his eyes, his lips, that firm, sexy jaw, and the fine wrinkles by his eyes. He looked tired.

"You scared me, baby," he whispered then softly kissed her cheek. She closed her eyes and wished to feel his lips against her lips and for his hands to take away the remnants of Jeff's, but instead he hugged her.

Kurt had big, wide, muscular shoulders and amazing abs like his brother. The feel of his arms was like a blanket of security wrapped around her.

"You're shaking, Mercedes. I swear, you're safe now."

She pulled back.

"I'm sorry. I don't know why I feel so scared. I freaked out a moment," she said and pulled all the way back and out of his hold. Kurt looked disappointed as he crossed his arms in front of his chest.

"Come on, let's get something to eat," Taylor told her and then Kurt motioned for her to walk ahead of him.

She did and when she got to her little kitchen, Warner was standing there. She hadn't seen him in forever, but he looked so good and he appeared monstrous in her small kitchen. He was just as tall as his brothers and a little more muscular up top than them.

"Mercedes," he said and then stepped closer to her. She lowered her head, clasping her hands in front of her in a submissive position. She waited for him to reprimand her, to scold her for being naive, stupid, unguarded. But it never came. Instead he lifted her chin with his fingers and held her gaze.

"Those will heal quickly, especially icing it a few times a day. We'll start after we eat," he said.

"I can do that. You really don't have to babysit me," she said to him.

"Mercedes, you were scared just now in your bedroom and we were in the next room. Don't be silly," Taylor told her as he reached for the big box of food from the bakery and deli in town.

"Jesus, you got enough food to feed an army," Kurt said but Warner just held her gaze.

"Seems our Mercedes has a lot of people who care about her. Mrs. Thomas hooked me up well when she learned that Kurt and I were bringing food over. There's lunch in there for later as well," he said.

She swallowed hard.

Warner didn't let up on his stare at her. She felt self-conscious.

"We all could have lost you."

"I know that. I'm sorry I was so stupid and didn't think anything bad even when my gut was alerting me to something strange. I haven't been on a date in forever."

He reached out and touched her waist. He drew her closer.

"You won't be going out on any other dates with any other men. We're going to watch over you, and keep you safe."

"You don't have to do that," she whispered, but his stare was so intense and his closeness got to her. Warner cupped her chin.

"We're going to make some changes, beginning with not hiding the way we feel about you and you about us. We want you. We have wanted you for quite some time and wanted to stake a claim but you kept sending the wrong signals and pushing us away. Not anymore. We've already made it official with Max and the others. Everyone will know that you belong to the Dawn men," he said so firmly it was like an order, or like she didn't know what but her body sure had a different response than her mind. Her pussy clenched, her nipples hardened, and she felt excited and aroused.

"Why are you saying this to me now? You've never even asked me out or showed an interest?"

"Because I was being stubborn and stupid. It doesn't matter. I'm here now."

"We're here now," Kurt said to her and she looked at all three of them.

But she was fearful. They were still the same men she worried couldn't commit to her, and that might break her heart and leave her scarred for life.

Besides that, she was feeling vulnerable, needy, and being in their arms, feeling their strong bodies so close made her want more of them. But this couldn't be good. She wrung her hands together and then felt Warner cover them with his. She gasped and looked up at him. He always intimidated her, put her on edge for so many reasons, but ultimately it was because he affected her.

"Don't give an answer now. Just think about it and let us show you we're sincere and that this was coming, even if you didn't want to admit it," Kurt added, making her turn toward him and causing Warner to release her hands. One glance at Warner and she could see he was angry, or maybe that was just his regular expression.

She didn't know what to say and Warner stepped back.

"Let's eat and then we'll talk some more," Taylor added to the conversation and she was fine with that. This was too heavy.

But as she opened her mouth to take a bite of the egg sandwich she felt the ache in her jaw. She closed her eyes and she saw Jeff hitting her.

"Are you okay? Does it hurt too much to eat?" Taylor asked, placing his hand on the back of her chair.

She opened her eyes and looked at him.

"I'll be fine, Taylor. Thank you," she whispered and then put the sandwich down and took a sip of the coffee. But she didn't feel hungry. She felt a myriad of emotions. She swallowed hard as she noticed the men had already finished their first egg sandwiches and were biting into their seconds. They were big men, with large appetites. The thought made her feel things and think things she shouldn't be thinking. She needed to get her mind off of this and ask some questions of her own. She had to gain back some character here and not be the damsel in distress, the trained female who set herself up for criminals to prey upon.

"So who do I speak to about my case? I mean who is in charge of finding those men who hurt me and tried to take me?" she asked.

They were all silent.

"That's not for you to worry about. We'll take care of everything along with Max and the rest of the department," Taylor told her.

"But I need to be kept in the loop. I want to know who those guys were and what they wanted."

"They wanted you," Kurt said in that tone of his.

She leaned back and swallowed hard.

"I want to know what they were after and if, well if I was the only one they were after or if my friends could be in danger."

"They were after you. That was obvious by their technique and the lengths at which they were willing to go to get you," Warner told her and then his cell phone buzzed. He read the text and then excused himself. She watched him walk into the living room.

"Listen, Mercedes, we're taking care of everything. Warner, Kurt, and I along with some close friends who do investigative work for a living are going to find these guys and get them. You don't need to worry about anything anymore because we're going to watch over you," Taylor said and reached out and caressed her cheek.

"I can take care of myself," she replied and stood up from the table. She didn't want them babying her. Now they thought she was weak.

She headed to the garbage and Kurt grabbed her wrist, stopping her.

"You need to eat."

She held his gaze. "I'm not hungry."

"You need to try and eat," he told her slowly and with conviction.

She stared at him and leaned a little closer. "I'm. Not. Hungry." She emphasized each word and pulled from his hold and walked toward the garbage. But when she turned around Kurt was standing there. He stepped toward her and she took a retreating step back. Her ass hit the counter.

Kurt stared down into her eyes. God, he was so good looking. She wanted so many things yet feared so many things. She'd never known men like this. Why did she feel like running, but also like letting go and letting them take whatever they wanted from her? It was ludicrous, irresponsible, and yet exciting, enticing, and she wanted to feel more.

* * * *

Kurt couldn't hold back. He'd waited so long to touch Mercedes, to kiss her and hold her in his arms, and the fact that he almost lost her overwhelmed him. He pressed closer, placed his hand on her hip and then reached up to cup her face and her hair. He tilted her head up toward him.

"Mercedes, I know you're scared. Hell, you scared the hell out of me last night. We could have lost you, and that isn't sitting right with any of us. Don't push us away because of that fear, or because you think we just suddenly grew feelings for you. We didn't." He looked at her expression and the way she appeared timid and accepting. He lowered his mouth closer to hers to test the water and see if she would let him kiss her. Just as his lips were about to kiss her, she closed her eyes and he felt relieved as he pressed his lips fully to hers.

He pulled her closer as he held her snugger against the island. She opened her mouth to his invasion and he explored her, pulling a moan from her, too. His cock hardened and he knew she felt it as she began to stop the kiss from continuing. She was sweet, sensual, and had a hell of a body. He slowly released her lips then cupped her cheeks between his hands.

"I've waited for a long time to do that. It was worth the wait," he said and she just stared at him. He released her cheeks and caressed her shoulders then her arms.

"You should really try to eat something." She shook her head.

Kurt took her hand and when they turned around Taylor was there staring at them and Warner looked upset.

Kurt wrapped his arm around Mercedes's waist, sensing that she wanted to pull away and try to leave and avoid Warner. His brother was intimidating to say the least but he needed to make his feelings known to Mercedes, or this wouldn't work and she wouldn't trust them.

Warner stepped closer.

* * * *

Warner didn't know why he reacted the way he did to seeing his brother Kurt kiss Mercedes like that. But it affected him, aroused him, had him practically hanging up on Gemini. He stepped closer, looking her over in the shorts and see-through T-shirt. Did she even know it was see-through? Probably not. She was classy, a lady, a woman who deserved everything including men who could cater to her every need and love her. Was he capable of love? Did he already love her, and that was why he was so fucking scared right now? He didn't know, but looking her over, seeing her eyes glisten with arousal, had him making his next move.

He was right in front of her, looking down at her petite frame, her big hazel eyes that just held his as she breathed unsteadily.

He reached out and took a strand of her lovely brown-red hair in his hands and let the silky strands pass through his fingers. He inhaled, smelling her shampoo and loving the scent of her. She looked so youthful, so special and gorgeous he felt unworthy to even touch her never mind want to possess her. But he couldn't resist. He needed to taste her, too, and to let her know that these feelings were strong and authentic.

He let his eyes roam over her body, her abundant breasts, her flat, firm waist and belly, and then her bare thighs. His cock hardened. He was so much bigger, they all were, and he could hurt her when all he wanted to do was take care of her and make her theirs.

"This isn't a game. We don't play games. Not when it comes to you and how we feel. I'm the reason why you were almost abducted last night." Her eyes widened.

"No, Warner. Why would you say that, or think that?" she asked him.

"If I hadn't been halfway across the world on some stupid job, running away from you and the feelings I have for you, then you would have been where you belong. In our bed, being our woman."

Her eyes widened and he couldn't say anymore. He had to taste her. He pulled her closer, his brother released her, and he swept his mouth over hers, kissing her deeply. When she ran her hands up against his chest, he deepened the kiss, lifted her up, and placed her onto the kitchen island. He caressed her everywhere his hands could reach. Over her back, under her ass, then back up to her back. He could wrap his arms fully around her and still have room because she was petite in comparison. He pressed closer, widening her thighs and getting a full taste of her. They were both kissing, trying to gain control of that kiss when he trailed his lips past her mouth to her neck and suckled hard.

"Oh God, Warner. Warner," she said his name, gripped his shirt at his shoulder with those delicate, small hands of hers that couldn't fight him off if she tried, and he thought about her attackers, the strikes she took, and how they tried to take her from him and his brothers. He grabbed her hips and pulled them forward as he thrust his body forward so she could feel how fucking hard she got him.

"Oh God," she moaned and he covered her mouth and kissed her again, stroked his tongue deeper, and then reached under her shirt and cupped her breast. She rocked her hips forward and he continued to massage her breast. They were firm, large, and felt like he imagined they would feel. Amazing. When he slowly began to release her lips he saw the expression on her face. Her lips were swollen, her face flushed, and her shirt dipped low enough to see the cleavage of her breasts and how well-endowed she was.

"You're going to be our woman. Hell, you already are, baby," he said and then he pulled his hand from under her shirt as Taylor stood by them. Taylor didn't hesitate. He reached out, cupped her cheeks, and kissed her fully on the mouth. That kiss grew wild, deeper in no time at all and when he pulled back Kurt was standing on the other side of her.

"What the hell just happened?" she whispered, staring at them.

Warner held her gaze with a firm one.

"You just got claimed, baby. It's official."

Chapter 5

"Have you found anything out at all?" Jeff asked Randall. Randall was one of the major players in the field and had done a lot of the online communications with buyers.

"One of the guys who intervened is a local deputy in Chance, where your little precious item lives. The other guy doesn't have shit on him, at least I wasn't able to find anything. He has like no record, just the fact that he is alive and lives in Chance, too," Randall said.

"Wonderful. Who the fuck would have expected cops to be hanging out there," Jeff said.

"You pushed her too soon. It would have been worth the effort to make another date or plans for a get-together," Damien said.

"You know as damn well as I do that time is of the essence. She wasn't attracted to either of us. She was so shy, reluctant to open up, and that just made her more appealing. I'm telling you, she's special. We don't have a lot of time to find these women, put them up for sale, and then grab them," Jeff countered.

"But still, she was sweet, shy, not experienced with men. It was obvious and you should have moved slower, seduced her better."

"Says you, Damien, who barely said a word to her. You could have helped."

"It doesn't matter how you screwed up, what matters is fixing it and getting our hands on her," Randall said to them.

"How the hell can we do that when our faces are plastered all over the news reports and every cop out there is looking for us?" Jeff asked.

"You have no choice. We need her," Randall replied.

"No, we don't. There were plenty of other women around there. Send in Carlos, Mickey D., or even Largo. They'll find some more product and we'll be good to go."

"Have you seen the numbers on the website? Have you even checked the live trending numbers on this woman?" Randall asked them.

"No," Damien said.

Randall walked over to the desk, typed some keys, and then turned the screen so they could see it.

Jeff was shocked. There were pictures of Mercedes. Ones they had taken and ones that were altered placing her in a string bikini. She was listed as a little southern virgin along with a description of her measurements, age, and height. But what caught his attention besides the curves of her body that were pretty damn accurate except her breast size. They were bigger in person. He stared at the screen. Could see the questions being asked, the bids being placed, and the scale that showed the final number and sale price for Mercedes was moving up on the screen.

"Six hundred thousand dollars?" Damien asked, sounding shocked.

Randall smiled.

"And rising as we speak."

"What are we going to do? They'll be cops all over her now, and we're screwed as is. We can't go anywhere," Damien said to Randall.

"We need to come up with some kind of plan to get this woman into our possession, or a lot of men are going to be pissed off, including the boss. He knows the deal. He knows that the two of you can't actually do the job this time. You both need to come up with a way to grab her. This one is taking a lot of attention away from the others we have listed. The boss believes that this bidding war will go over a million dollars. So think of something," Randall told them and Jeff stared at the screen.

How the hell was he going to get his hands on Mercedes? Who could he send in, and how could they get away with it?

* * * *

Mercedes wondered when they would leave. It was getting late. She was tired and had aches and pains and she wanted rest so that she could go back to work tomorrow. She needed the money.

She looked at Warner as he worked on the laptop communicating with whomever he knew that was working the case. Kurt was on his I-pad and texting things every so often, and Luke sat right next to her, flipping through the channels on the television set.

Her eyelids were getting heavy as she tried staying awake and wondering what it would be like to have the three of them with her like this all the time. She would never be alone. If she needed a hug, a conversation, anything at all, one of them would be there. Was that the way this worked?

She closed her eyes and thought about the others. Her friends spoke of different aspects to ménage relationships so often, and Mercedes paid attention. Despite the fact that she didn't ever want to rely on someone or feel she had to.

God, I'm so tired.

* * * *

Taylor watched Mercedes sleeping. She looked so beautiful. He only wished she didn't have the bruises on her cheek and her jaw. Her feet were curled up underneath her and her hands under her cheek as she slept against the throw pillow. Her home was neat and she had very little items around. He often wondered what her place might look like. What her bedroom looked like. What she slept in, if anything at all.

He felt his dick harden beneath his pants and he shifted. He reached over and caressed her thigh. She scrunched up her face and made a sound like she was afraid or uncomfortable and then she jerked. Her eyes popped open. She looked around the room and locked gazes with him.

"You're okay," Taylor told her.

"I know," she said, sounding kind of snappy.

She sat up, ran her fingers through her hair, and then swallowed hard.

"I'm sorry, but I'm tired. I need to go to bed. So, I guess I'll see you tomorrow maybe?" she asked as she stood up.

"We're not leaving you," Kurt told her.

She looked at him as Taylor took her hand then stood up.

"I'll walk you to bed.

"You don't have to stay. I'll need to get up early for work tomorrow," she told them.

"You can take another day. Max won't mind," Warner told her.

"But I mind. I don't miss work. I need the money, so it's not your decision, it's mine," She said and headed toward her bedroom.

As she got to her room and was about to close the door, Warner was there. He pressed the door open. His large palm against the white wooden door looked huge. Hell, he was huge all over.

He stepped forward into her room and she stepped back until her calves touched the edge of the bed.

"It is my business. It became my business the moment we decided to make you our woman. It's even more so my business, because some assholes tried to take you," he said and then pulled her close. She gasped as she felt his hand at her lower back then his other hand move under her hair by her neck and cup her head. He tilted her head up toward him.

"We're not leaving you. As we discussed earlier, things are going to change because you are our woman. You want us, like we want you, right, Mercedes?" he asked her and she didn't hesitate. She nodded her head. His brown eyes roamed over the cleavage of her chest. Then to her lips right before he kissed her.

That kiss grew deeper very quickly. Then she felt herself being lowered over the bed and her back hit the comforter with ease as Warner held her.

He explored her mouth as he spread her thighs with his one leg and then maneuvered his fingers to her waist. He pressed his fingers under the elastic waistband and she wanted to feel his touch so badly she ached down there, more than her cheek and jaw ached.

She knew if she let him touch her there, stroke her pussy and make her come, that she would want more. She would want to have sex for the very first time and she was just too insecure and scared.

But Warner, Taylor, and Kurt did things to her. They touched her heart and made her want them. She wanted all they were willing to give and for however long.

She gripped his wrist as she pulled from his mouth.

"Please don't, Warner. I'm not ready," she said to him. His expression was dark, and he looked older, experienced, and she wondered if she should let him touch her down there so that he wouldn't know how inexperienced she was.

"This body is going to belong to my brothers and I. We will never hurt you or do something to you to scare you or make you feel bad."

"I know that. I understand. But everything you're telling me is new. I need slow, Warner," she told him, even though her body wanted fast. It wanted her to beg for sex, for mercy. For whatever a woman begs for when a man plays her pussy strings like an instrument.

He stared at her, running his palm from her belly to her breast. He rubbed his thumb back and forth over her nipple. Despite wearing a bra she felt it harden and she parted her lips.

"Your body knows, Mercedes. You're so responsive to my touch. Don't fight it no matter what your fears are, we'll work through them," he said and lowered his lips to hers and kissed her gingerly.

She hadn't expected the pinch to her nipple, or the flow of cream that had her lifting her pelvis up against his waist.

He pulled back and stared into her eyes.

"I can't wait to explore this body. To watch my fingers, my lips, my cock arouse you and make you come." She started breathing heavier and she licked her lower lip only for Warner to kiss her again and pull that lower lip into his mouth then release it. He was so experienced, so capable.

"Oh God, Warner. I've never heard you talk so much," she said as she tried to gain some control of her libido.

"You bring it out in me," he replied and then kissed her jaw, her neck and then her shoulder.

"You travel a lot for work. How can you be with me so much?" she asked him.

He held her gaze and caressed the hair from her cheek.

"Things are changing, Mercedes. For me, too, and for my brothers. We're going to make sure that you're safe, that you're provided for, and that you never feel alone or unloved," he said and then kissed the corner of her mouth. God, she wanted to believe it. She wanted to buy into the whole thing but she was scared.

"You can't make promises like that."

He rose up slightly and held her gaze.

"What I say is true. I'm a man of my word," he said.

Every instinct told her that he was being honest. But she had concerns, reservations, anxiety about opening up her heart and getting hurt.

"You're doing a lot of thinking, but you're not talking. Explain to us what your fears are and we'll work through them," Warner said.

Taylor and Kurt sat down on the bed. Kurt caressed her hair and held her gaze.

"I can't," she whispered. Kurt's expression changed. He looked hurt, maybe a little angry. These men were out of her league, older, set in their ways, and dominant. Did she really want to open herself up to them?

When she thought about their kisses she believed she did.

"Maybe if you tell me more about the three of you?" she suggested.

"And you'll tell us more about you?" Warner asked, adjusting his body so little of his weight was on her as he lay with his thigh over her thigh and between her legs.

"Okay," she said.

"What would you like to know?" Kurt asked her.

Suddenly all her questions were at her lips.

"Have you ever been in a committed relationship? Have the three of you ever shared a woman? Do you have parents, any family? Where do you go when you leave for months at a time. Oh, will you order me around and tell me what to do? Is that part of the control thing? Because I've been alone for years now and to tell you the truth, I'm used to only taking care of myself and I don't really trust people. I'm very shy, too, and get intimidated easily. I don't like that feeling."

Warner gently placed his fingers over her lips as he smiled. His brothers chuckled.

She felt embarrassed for rambling on the way she did but as soon as she asked the first question, she had to ask more.

"Okay, one, I believe the three of us have never been in a committed relationship. We've always been busy with our careers and traveling," Warner told her.

"And never met a woman that drew all of our interest at the same time," Kurt added.

"We have shared women before, but things were missing. It only clarified that we wanted to share a woman and that would be our ultimate ideal relationship," Taylor said to her as he caressed her hair.

She locked onto his hazel eyes and exhaled. He was so good-looking.

Warner caressed her thigh as he leaned on his elbow and watched her.

"We have parents. Two dads and a mom. They don't live far from here," Taylor said and she looked at him and smiled.

"You're lucky then, and to have two dads. That's pretty amazing, and also so odd for me to think about," she replied.

"Why is that?" Kurt asked, taking her hand and bringing it to his lips. He kissed her knuckles and held her gaze.

The move caused her breasts to lift higher and she felt them swell with desire. These three men were so good-looking. So sexy and masculine. She felt like such a peanut. Yet, she felt sexy. Or at least she hoped she looked sexy, lying here with three men, with Taylor, Warner, and Kurt on her bed. This was a first for her. She'd never let a man in her bedroom. Did she want them here? Was it too intimate?

Warner clutched her chin and held her gaze, drawing her complete attention to him.

"There you go again, thinking and not talking. Don't be afraid. Tell us about your parents, about your childhood, about what brought you to Chance," he said to her then released her chin. She rolled over so that she was on her back and really wouldn't have to face one of them.

"My parents were very sick. They had high blood pressure, diabetes and bone deterioration to just name a few of their ailments. Most of high school is a blur, because I basically went to school then headed home to take care of my parents. Within those four years their medical conditions got worse. They couldn't function without my help and were wheel chair bound. It was the worst years of my life. To have to watch them suffer, be in pain, and lose limbs and eventually their sight from the diabetes. They deteriorated quickly and first my mom passed, and then a month later, my dad."

"That's terrible. Didn't you have any family around to help you?" Taylor asked.

She shook her head.

"I'm an only child. My parents hadn't expected to have children. I think I was a mistake but of course my mom always said I was a blessing," she admitted and then felt the tears in her eyes. She always felt self-conscious about that. Knowing her parents hadn't intended to have her and then her mom got pregnant.

Warner caressed her thigh and gave her hip bone a squeeze. "Definitely a blessing," he said and she smiled. His comment made her feel good.

"So what did you do when they passed away?" Taylor asked.

"They had some money saved but not much. I had to sell the house and broke even. I did sell all the furniture and it was enough to pay for some classes at the local community college when I graduated. But times were tough. I really didn't know what to do and there was nowhere to turn so I did what I thought was best," she said and remembered the long scary nights on the streets and the few times she stayed in the shelter were even scarier.

Kurt covered her hand and squeezed it.

"What did you do to survive on your own?"

She held his gaze. Those blue eyes of his touched her heart and she found herself explaining everything to them.

"You lived on the streets and in shelters?" Warner asked sounding angry.

"I didn't have much of a choice. It was for about a month or so. I really don't remember and I don't like talking about it. When I landed the small job on the college campus, it was a lifesaver. I would stay in one of the lab rooms. There were professors that worked all night long and they left the doors unlocked. I was able to sneak into a closet or set up things in a corner in the back, and no one noticed. Or maybe they did and they just let me get away with it. I don't know. But it was better, safer than the shelters or the streets. I would shower in the girl's locker room and people always left things around like shampoo, conditioner, even clothes. It was tough but then the hours increased with the job on campus."

"My God, baby, you're incredible. A survivor," Kurt told her and then he leaned forward and kissed her softly on the lips.

When he pulled back she felt even more aroused. She loved when they kissed her. She loved the feel of their masculine lips against hers. The way their big strong muscles wrapped around her and made her feel safe. She still never really felt safe at night.

"How did you end up in Chance?" Kurt asked her.

"Mrs. Peters worked at the community college with me. She told me about the job, and set up the interview with Max and then the board."

Warner was playing with the hem of her shirt. He lifted it higher. The feel of his large, heavy hand made her core tingle and her pussy tighten. His fingers stroked over her skin and she tightened up only for him to move closer and kiss her lips.

"We'll have to thank Mrs. Peters," he said when he released her lips and then kissed her again.

He took his time tasting her, pulling on her lower lip then drawing her full lips into another smoldering kiss. It was too much. He was breaking her down. Weakening her defenses. His hand moved upward and cupped her breast.

She grabbed onto his hand and gasped as he released her lips. His eyes roamed over her chest and the cleavage that showed.

"You're quite voluptuous, Mercedes. I want to explore you a little more."

She was breathing heavier.

"Perhaps we can assist," Taylor said and then took her hand and brought it up above her head and he kissed the top. She watched him, taking her eyes off of Warner a moment until she felt Kurt take her other hand and bring it up above her head. He kissed along her skin, down her arm to her inner elbow, making her giggle and tighten up.

"Someone is ticklish," he said and then suckled against the underside of her wrist.

Warner's lips touched her belly and then moved upward.

"Warner," she practically moaned.

"Easy, baby, just exploring and clarifying things," he said as he pressed a palm up over her breast as he used his fingers from his other hand to undo her bra.

"About the liking to have control part you asked about," Kurt told her, and she thought she might pass out she was so aroused.

Warner lifted her top, revealing her full, round breasts to him and his brothers.

"Sweet Jesus, Mercedes. Where you been hiding those, baby?" Taylor teased then ran the palm of his free hand down over her shoulder and to a breast. Kurt cupped the other one as Taylor played with the nipple and remained holding her arm above her head.

She wiggled her hips and shook and nearly screamed it was torturous.

"Please. Oh God, you guys are too much. Too wild," she said to them.

"You bring it out in us, baby," Warner whispered as he blew warm breath against her left nipple as Taylor held part of it forward for his brother like an offering.

As Warner stuck out his tongue, Taylor released her breasts and Warner suckled the nipple. She watched his cheeks cave in and then go back to normal. He twirled his tongue around her breast as Kurt released her other breast and Warner cupped it and massaged it.

Having all three men touch her like this at once was overwhelming, arousing, so damn wild she started not to care about anything but letting go and giving in.

It was overwhelming and she felt her pussy clench then release a small bit of cream.

"Warner, please. Oh God that feels so good," she said and tilted her head back. When she lifted her hips, Kurt reached down and pressed his hand under the elastic of her shorts. Before she could react his fingers stroked up into her wet cunt.

She lost it.

"Oh. My. God," she said and she came.

* * * *

Kurt couldn't believe it. One touch, a few pulls on her nipples, and a finger to her cunt, and Mercedes was practically shooting up off the bed.

He nodded toward Taylor to hold her hands above her head and he did as Kurt began to push her panties and shorts down.

"No, wait. Oh God please," she said, sounding scared.

She wiggled and tried pulling her hands down.

"Oh God we can't. You can't. I'm not ready. I don't really know you that well. I mean it feels great and oh God, we have to stop." She carried on, making Taylor chuckle.

"It's okay, Mercedes. We just want to make you feel good and explore this sexy body," Taylor told her as he lifted her wrists, bent over, and kissed them.

"But I—what are you going to do?" she asked, sounding so innocent.

"Well I know what I want to do. I want to taste your sweet cream and make you come. You are going to look sexy and beautiful when you come. I just know it," Kurt said as he eased her panties and shorts down and off of her.

Warner reached over and caressed her inner thigh. She shook and looked so scared.

She locked gazes with Kurt.

"You're safe, and you belong to me and my brothers. We want to explore what's ours," he told her then leaned up and kissed her deeply. When he felt her relax a little he pulled back and slowly slid toward the bottom of the bed as Warner kissed her next. When he was done, Kurt pressed her legs apart, stared at her perfectly manicured pussy, and licked his lips.

"I can't wait to taste you," he said then eased down over her pussy. He used his tongue and lips to arouse her, to get her to relax and just let go. Here and there he added a digit or two and drew out soft purrs and then moans of pleasure from her.

She tasted so good, smelled delicious, and then he felt her rock her hips.

"That's right, baby. Just let go and let us have all of you," Warner said, cupping her breast and pinching the nipple.

She looked like a goddess spread out before them. Taylor held her arms above her head and suckled her inner wrists against the sensitive spot. Warner was feasting on her breasts while Kurt thrust fingers in and out of her pussy until she moaned a release. Her cream poured from her cunt and he fell between her thighs and licked and suckled what he could.

"Sweet mother you're so damn responsive. Fuck, you got my dick so hard," Kurt told her, pulling away from her pussy, lips moist from her cream, and she gasped. Her hazel eyes grew wide as saucers as she stared at Kurt. She closed her thighs, locking Kurt, Taylor, and Warner out.

"Let go, Taylor. Please," she said.

Taylor did immediately. They all heard the fear, the worry in her tone.

"What is it, baby?" Kurt asked as he sat up.

She tried sitting up to grab her shorts.

"Here. Let me help you," he offered and she slid back into her panties and shorts.

She then pulled her shirt down.

"What is it? What's wrong?" Warner asked her.

"That was too much too soon. Overwhelming," she said and then ran a nervous hand through her hair.

Warner smiled then touched her chin and tilted her head up toward him.

"Not too much. Never too much. You're perfect, and if you need more time to get to know us that's fine. We're not going anywhere," he told her and Taylor then Kurt nodded.

Kurt felt such a need, a possessive desire in him, he lowered half over her body and kissed her deeply. When he felt her fingers run through his hair and hold him tight, he was relieved. He would be as patient as he could be. But he knew it wouldn't last long.

Chapter 6

When Mercedes entered the sheriff's department, she was greeted by everyone. It felt so good to be cared for and to live in a town like Chance. Over the past year she had seen lots of people helping one another out and knew the town was special. But feeling the love, the concern from the citizens of Chance as well as her fellow coworkers, truly touched her heart.

But as she headed toward her desk after receiving some hugs, her eyes landed on the yellow bouquet of flowers. She panicked and stopped short. She instantly turned around and grabbed onto Taylor's arms.

"Taylor, the flowers. Oh my God, someone sent them to me the other day and I have no idea who. What if it were those men? What if they were watching me at the supermarket and here in town?"

He smiled softly and caressed her arms.

"It's okay, sweetheart. It wasn't them. I already checked it out. You're safe here, too," he said and she looked at him strangely. She felt strangely, but before she could question him the sheriff called his name.

"Taylor, I need you in my office a minute."

Taylor nodded his head and then looked back at Mercedes. He held her gaze as he reached over and cupped her cheek. "You're the one that said you wanted to head back to work. I'll catch you later. I won't be far away. Okay?"

She nodded her head. He leaned down and kissed her lips softly and she felt so much better. As he walked toward Max's office, Thelma hurried over.

"Woman, you have got to tell me the details about how Taylor and Kurt showed up at that bar and rescued you. If that isn't fate, then I don't know what is," Thelma said.

"Fate?" Mercedes asked as she walked around her desk. She still was feeling uneasy about not knowing who sent the flowers, and who was obviously watching her in the grocery store last week.

"Yes, fate. Those damn men have been wanting you for quite some time. They've turned down so many offers of dates. You're one lucky lady and they sure are three lucky men."

"Turning down dates?" she asked.

"Oh yes, I've had to help some of these men around here, Taylor included, dodge a few calls from pestering females. Seems your Taylor is quite the catch. But that's all over now. They're all yours and no woman can even think of trying to push in."

"Thelma, I need you."

One of the deputies called out Thelma's name and she smiled wide, excused herself, and hurried toward her desk.

Mercedes thought about what Thelma said about the women and she felt a bit jealous. The Dawn men were hers as she was theirs. As soon as she talked to her friends and gained a bit more confidence, she would let her guard down and let them make love to her. Just thinking about it made her feel all aroused and a nervous wreck. They were older, more experienced men. Maybe they wouldn't want a virgin, but instead a woman who knew her way around a man's body and how to please him?

She felt sick and then Taylor walked out of the sheriff's office, gave her a wink and headed toward the front door.

Instantly her emotions changed again. She felt giddy, safe, and pretty important that she snagged the Dawn men as hers. Thinking that made her feel excited yet scared out of her mind. She needed to focus on work. The other things would come later.

* * * *

"Okay, so let's talk this through," Adele said to Mercedes as Alicia and Marlena took their seats around them and sipped their sweet tea.

"Please lower your voices. I don't want the guys to know or anyone for that matter. It's personal and I really need to figure out if I'm ready," Mercedes said to them.

"You are ready. You've been ready for months. We've been around you when one of the Dawn brothers show up," Alicia stated.

"You get all quiet, and you stare at them, probably absorbing all those muscles and fantasizing about how they'll feel when you get an opportunity to explore them," Adele added.

They chuckled.

"I don't stare at them," Mercedes said as she ran her finger along the rim of the sweet tea.

Adele, Alicia, and Marlena chuckled. Marlena covered Mercedes's hand. "It's okay, sweetie. We've all done it with our men and still do. You like them, and there's nothing wrong with that," she added.

"I do like them, but I've never even had a boyfriend. Think about that. I've never let a man get close to me like that," she whispered and Adele knew what she meant.

"That's nothing to be ashamed of, or uncertain about. It's special. Being able to offer three men you love and who love you, a part of you, hell, all of you, like you've never given to anyone else is so special. They care so much about you, Mercedes," Marlena said.

"They only started really caring after Taylor and Kurt saw me nearly get abducted."

"That's not true. They were there watching over you, being jealous that you were on another date and ensuring that you were safe. I'd say that is pretty obvious they have had their eyes on you and wanted you for a while," Adele said to her.

"I know you're right, but this is what I keep doing. I keep minimizing what I know is real and focusing on only trusting me to take care of me. You know what I mean?" Mercedes asked them. They all nodded.

"It's time to let that wall down and allow Kurt, Taylor, and Warner to love you and care for you. They're letting walls down, too, you know," Alicia added.

"She's right. Kurt and especially Warner would disappear for months at a time on missions or government jobs. Dangerous jobs from what we've all heard through gossip."

"I know, Adele. Warner blames himself for me getting into the situation. He said if he hadn't been running away from his feelings for me, then I wouldn't have been there. I would have been with them in their bed, making love," she said.

Adele whistled low.

"Hot damn. So the quiet, strong, killer eyes Warner is a bit romantic. Interesting," Marlena teased.

"Follow your heart, Mercedes. It's the advice you gave all of us when we considered ménage relationships with our men. Look how happy we all are. We want that for you, too. You deserve it," Alicia told her.

Mercedes smiled and Adele felt happy for her. She was part of her family, too. They all were, and she wanted Mercedes safe and well loved, just like the rest of her friends. The Dawn brothers were perfect for Mercedes, but she had to accept them. Adele hoped Mercedes followed her heart. She worried about her, and especially about these men that were still out there. What if they returned? What if Mercedes didn't let down her guard and trust the Dawn men? Would those men seek her out again and succeed?

She prayed not, as she listened to her friends talk and try to ease Mercedes's mind about sex and trusting her men. They really were all best friends who could talk about anything. Adele had never been happier, and she wanted that for Mercedes, too.

* * * *

"Where are we going?" Mercedes asked Taylor as they headed in his truck toward the edge of town.

"Our place. Kurt cooked dinner and we thought it would be nice to get together and let you see where we live. You don't mind, do you?" Taylor asked. She had her hands clasped on her lap and she felt anxious. She was still wearing her work clothes. A knee-length floral skirt with hints of lavender, and a lavender camisole and matching sheer overlying blouse.

Taylor reached over and covered her hand with his.

"How did everything go at lunch? Did it feel good to see your friends and talk a bit?" he asked. He had no idea.

She smiled.

"It's always nice to get together with my friends. When I first arrived in Chance I didn't know anyone. It's funny how we all met and became so close. They're like family to me," she said and looked out the window.

"Come here," he whispered as he drove up the long driveway and then parked the truck as she slid closer. He placed it in park and held her gaze. Taylor cupped her cheeks and stared into her eyes.

"We care about you so much. We hope real soon you'll consider us family. That you'll let us take care of you, support you, and protect you always."

"I want that, too," she admitted.

He looked intense but pleased.

Slowly Taylor kissed her lips. That kiss grew deeper, wilder in no time as they fought for control. He lifted her onto his lap and dipped her slightly as he ran his hand up her skirt and caressed her thigh.

She was aroused, needy, and she parted her thighs slightly, giving his fingers access to her panties.

She shivered as his thick, hard digit caressed over her mound. The friction made her squirm and moan as she cupped his cheek and pressed her breasts closer to his chest.

He ran a finger along her waist, under the elastic of her panties, and then maneuvered them beneath the material.

She moaned softly and then felt his knuckles press her thighs wider. She widened her thighs and he immediately pressed closer. She felt his finger trace her pussy lips then press right up into her wet cunt. She lifted her feet a little higher, giving him better access to her cunt as she moaned into his mouth. His arm flexed, and jerked in and out from between her thighs. Her body tightened and she knew she would come.

"Oh God, Taylor. Taylor," she moaned after she pulled her lips from his. He suckled her neck and she tilted her head back against the door window and thrust her hips to his finger strokes.

"That's it, baby. Let me have it. Let go and come for me," he ordered her and she grabbed his wrist as she came. She shook and felt her body explode and then he pulled out his fingers and hugged her to him.

"You're perfect. You're mine, baby. God, you make me crazy."

"Oh my God. That was—that felt so good," she whispered as he helped her fix her skirt. He ran his palm along her belly then cupped her breasts.

"You have one hell of a body, Mercedes. It's going to belong to my brothers and I really soon. You're going to trust us, and we're going to be one family, together forever."

Before she could respond he kissed her again and then opened the door.

She was shocked to feel strong arms take her from Taylor.

"Kurt?" she whispered. He looked angry, intense, kind of furious. She was embarrassed and felt guilty for some strange reason. Like she just got caught having sex in a truck with her boyfriend.

"You're just filled with surprises huh, baby?" he asked as he lowered her feet to the ground but not before he kissed her deeply. As he set her feet down on the ground, he ran his hand under her skirt and then gave her ass a tap.

"Keep that pussy wet and ready. I'm having a taste of you before dinner."

She nearly came in her panties from his words. But he took her hand and Taylor placed his arm over her shoulder as they headed into their large home.

* * * *

"I'm sorry, man. Fucking Slick stumbled across it on a fluke search. I don't know what you want to do."

"I want to get these guys and I want to fucking kill them." Warner raised his voice.

"That's understandable, Warner. Those are pictures of your woman posted on there. They got scumbags bidding over a million dollars for her. Those numbers are going up. You know what this means."

"Yeah I fucking know what it means. They're going to come for her. They want my woman to sell. That isn't going to fucking happen. Have Slick look deeper. There has to be a way to find the host to this bidding site and the owner. Don't fucking tip them off that we're onto them. Record their site for evidence later. If I wind up hunting down these fucking assholes and killing them, at least the government will know why."

"We're right there with you guys. We'll help you protect Mercedes. We'll do everything in our power."

"Thanks, Gemini."

Warner rubbed his light beard on his chin and cheeks as he stared at the pictures of Mercedes. The ones in a bikini were obviously superimposed. His woman had a better body and bigger breasts. What stood out more were the numbers on a scale that kept rising. It was over a million dollars and rising to purchase her. Like she was some object, some material thing money could buy. It made him sick and the thought that they could be looking for her enraged him.

She belonged to him and his brothers. No one else.

"Warner?"

He heard his brother Kurt's voice and he turned around in his seat.

"What the fuck is that?" Kurt asked and walked into the room. He stared at the picture.

"Southern virgin angel? That's Mercedes."

Warner filled him in on the information.

"We have to find these sons of bitches. We need to notify everyone so they know these losers are out there hunting her and perhaps other women," Kurt said.

"Not perhaps," Warner replied and then clicked onto another screen. There was a list of other women. It showed their pictures and the prices they sold at or were being sold for. It was disgusting.

"I'm calling it in. This is a federal situation, too. There are more than a hundred women on this site. There are probably other sites, too."

"Mercedes? How do we protect her?"

"By keeping her close. Like in our bed," Warner said and logged off the computer then stood up. They headed out of the room and when they got to the kitchen Mercedes was slightly bent over the counter leaning next to Taylor looking at a magazine.

"This is the recipe?" she asked him.

"Yup, Kurt is a good cook. We'll see if it tastes that good," Taylor teased.

Warner watched Mercedes. He couldn't help but to think about the pictures of her and the word *virgin* in bold letters. How would the men know that? Could they just be saying that to cause hype? Could Mercedes be a virgin?

"Warner?" she whispered his name and he tightened up.

"What did you tell those men about you when you were on your date?" he asked, sounding hard.

She didn't respond right away. His question shocked her.

"The men, what questions did they ask you and how did you respond? Did you tell them anything personal?"

"No. Nothing at all. Conversation didn't run smoothly."

He squinted his eyes a moment. His mind was traveling in so many directions, but it kept ending up with needing Mercedes. He wouldn't let these men find her and take her from him and his brothers. He wouldn't let them touch what was his.

He pressed up against her back. She tightened up.

"I missed you," he said to her and leaned forward. She tilted her head up and sideways to touch her lips to his.

He ran his hands along her waist and gave her hips a squeeze.

"You look beautiful. As always," he said after releasing her lips.

She turned in his arms and he lifted her up and placed her onto the island in the kitchen.

He pressed her legs apart and she gripped his shoulders, holding his gaze.

"Warner?" she asked and he pulled her closer, his mind on the images, the price on her body, the body that would be theirs.

He kissed her deeply and she kissed him back. As he lowered her down, her back touched the granite island counter and he pushed her skirt up.

"You belong to us. Every fucking inch of you," he said.

He lowered as he pushed her panties aside and pressed a finger to her moist cunt. In and out he stroked her pussy. Then he added a second digit before he lowered his mouth to her pussy and took over. He swirled his tongue around and nipped at her clit. She rocked her hips and he reached down to unzip his pants.

"I need you, baby. We all do. Are you on the pill?" he asked and she gasped. She sat up and gripped his shoulders.

He grabbed her thighs, stopping her from pulling back. He pressed them against his thighs.

"Don't push us away."

"I'm not. I want you, too. I just need a minute, and not here. Not on the table. Not..."

She didn't complete her sentence as she lowered her head. He cupped her chin.

"What is it? What are you not telling us?" he asked as Taylor and Kurt stood by them.

She tilted her head up toward them.

"Why I was holding back. Why I had trouble letting my guard down with you guys, until now that is."

"Why?" Taylor asked her.

"I've never had sex before. I never even had a boyfriend because I was so busy taking care of my parents and then trying to survive and not live permanently on the streets. You're so experienced and it scares me because I don't want to get hurt. I want...I want forever," she said as a tear rolled down her cheek.

Warner's heart soared with such love and desire he couldn't resist kissing her.

He pulled her close, kissed her deeply, and then carried her out of the kitchen.

"The bed. Your first time should be on a bed, surrounded by the three of us loving you together," he told her after he released her lips.

She hugged him tight and kissed his neck as he carried her out of the kitchen, his brothers in tow.

"I need that, Warner. I want all three of you so badly it scares me. I feel desperate."

"So do I, Mercedes. So do I," he said.

Warner placed her feet down onto the carpet.

He slowly helped her undress and she helped him undress. Taylor and Kurt stripped, too, and Kurt walked over toward the side of the bed.

"Going slow is going to be torture," he told her as he took in the sight of her voluptuous body. Her complexion was tan, almost olive. Her hazel eyes held his as he reached out and cupped both breasts. She felt full, firm, and he ran his thumb along the nipple then pinched.

Her lips parted. "You are such a stunning woman. We're honored to be your firsts and to have the opportunity to love you," he said to her and stepped closer, keeping one hand on her breast, manipulating the nipple and the other pressed over her mound and then he dipped a finger into her cunt.

She gripped his wrist.

"Let go. Give me complete control. Give me all of you," he told her and she let her arms fall to her sides as she gasped an held his gaze.

Kurt stepped in behind her. He reached underneath and cupped her breasts.

"Bring her back, Kurt. I need a taste," he said.

Kurt sat down on the bed taking Mercedes with him and then maneuvering her thighs over his thighs spreading her wide.

Taylor rubbed his hands together.

"She's wet and ready for us," he whispered.

"That she is," Warner said and lowered to his knees.

He pressed her thighs open with his palms, caressed them, massaging them before he moved his mouth over her pussy. She wiggled and moaned as he ate her cream, pinched her clit, and aroused her to the extreme. When he ran his tongue along her anus she gasped, bucked upward, and then pressed down.

"Every part of you is going to belong to us. We're claiming all of you tonight. Do you understand?" he asked, holding her gaze as he flicked his tongue back and forth against her clit.

"Yes...yes. Oh god," she stuttered and he delved his tongue deeper.

Kurt cupped her breasts and pulled on her nipples.

"That means this virgin pussy, your virgin ass, and this virgin mouth, Mercedes. You're going to be filled with our cocks as we claim every inch of you. I need you. I want you so badly my cock is throbbing right now," Kurt confessed.

"I've got the lube ready," Taylor said from the side and he caressed her hair from her cheeks.

Mercedes lips were parted and she was rocking her hips.

Warner could tell she was getting aroused and ready to come. He licked at her anus again and then as he licked her pussy lips he pressed a finger to her anus.

"Oh God, Warner. Warner." She pushed forward but Kurt held her back.

He added another digit to her pussy, thrusting fingers into both holes. He used his palm to grip her thighs.

"Look at me, Mercedes. Look at me," Warner ordered firmly.

Her eyes darkened and she widened them.

"You're our woman. From this day on, no holding back. No keeping secrets, no being afraid of us, of this relationship. We're not going anywhere."

"Yes, Warner. Yes, I want that. I need you," she cried out.

He pulled his fingers from her ass and cunt and then suckled her clit hard. Mercedes cried out as she wiggled and came.

* * * *

"One at a time and then together for her first times," Mercedes heard Warner tell them.

Kurt massaged her thighs as he lifted them up and off his thighs and then he placed her onto the bed. In a flash Warner was between her legs, stroking his cock and holding her gaze.

She stared at him, absorbing his sexy body, the hard definition of muscles mixed with some scars. There were what appeared to be deep, healed gashes, thin slices, and something that looked fairly new against his shoulder.

She reached up and touched it. He turned to the right and kissed her wrist.

"I almost lost this chance with you. That part of my life is over. You come first, Mercedes. Now. Always." He caressed along her thighs and then aligned his cock with her pussy.

She ran her hands up and down his arms, not asking what exactly his statement meant but understanding that his proclamation came from the heart.

"I want you," he told her.

"Take me. I want you, too. All three of you," she said.

She was scared, and she couldn't hide it. She'd waited far too long to give up this part of her and as she absorbed the feel of Warner's hands holding her hips, as she inhaled his cologne, took in the sight of his masculinity, sex appeal, and maturity, he eased his cock between her wet folds. He paused, teeth clenched, eyes glued to hers.

"I feel it. You're ours."

He pressed deeper then thrust completely into her, making her gasp and close her eyes. She felt it, too. That thin piece of skin as it disappeared with the thrust of Warner's muscle.

He leaned over her, hugged her to him, and began to rock his hips. With every in and out stroke she lost her breath. He was so big, and he felt so large and heavy over her. But she loved the sensation. She loved feeling protected and she showed him.

Mercedes licked along his neck and bit gently on a sensitive spot. He moaned and then lifted up and she gripped his arms as best she could while he began to set a pace. In and out he stroked her pussy and it felt wonderful.

"You're so big, Warner. I can hardly breathe when you're inside of me."

"You'll get used to it. Just as you'll get used to all of us inside of you," he told her and then kissed her deeply before she could freak out.

As he lifted up, he pulled her legs higher and over his thighs. He thrust in and out as he used his palms to rub along her abs to her breasts where he pulled and massaged her breasts and nipples. She was moaning, feeling the tension inside her building and building. She reached out and ran her palms against his chest and he hissed then thrust harder.

She pulled on his nipple and he growled low.

"Watch it, missy, or I won't go easy on you," he warned.

"Easy? You're going easy on me?" she asked.

He smirked at her in a very mysterious way and then he lifted her thighs higher, up over his shoulders as he plunged deeply into her cunt. The bed rocked and dipped and she cried out her first release then wiggled and moaned while Warner continued to stroke his cock into her. One, two, three more strokes and he shoved deeply, moaned, and came inside of her.

As he lowered her thighs, he covered her body and kissed every inch of her he could. Along her neck, her shoulder, and then to her lips.

"Mine," he said and squeezed her hips then cupped her breasts before he kissed each tip.

She giggled and lay there feeling really good and really happy.

"My turn," Taylor whispered as Warner pulled out of her, making her moan and then exhale.

Taylor pressed between her thighs and immediately stroked a finger up into her cunt.

"Taylor," she gasped and he thrust his fingers in and out.

"Just making sure that you're nice and wet so we don't hurt you," he said and then pulled his fingers out and replaced them with his cock. He pressed the tip to her entrance and then held her gaze.

"You want me, like I want you," he asked.

"Yes," she said, holding his gaze. His blue eyes sparkled with desire and mischief. She almost chuckled.

She ran her hands up and down his chest as he eased his cock deeper. He went slowly. Too slowly as she wiggled, wanting, needing the deep sensation she felt with Warner.

"Please, Taylor. I need it," she said to him.

He looked a little shocked at her confession but then he eased deeper and deeper and then pulled out and thrust back into her cunt. From there on out she held on tight and gasped for breath, for every stroke from Taylor's cock collided against the internal muscles and he felt so hard, it made her come and scream out his name.

She shook her head side to side and then cried out as he pinched her nipple. When she felt his finger go over her anus and press against the puckered hole she lost it. Mercedes cried out as she came.

"So fucking hot. She needs a cock in her ass. She wants it," Taylor said to his brothers but held her gaze as he lifted her thighs higher and pounded into her pussy until he shook and came inside of her.

Taylor hugged her to him and kissed her tenderly. He eased out of her and Kurt was there to pull her into his arms and lift her up onto his body. She straddled him and held his gaze, her eyes locked onto his muscular chest and the smoothness of his skin. She couldn't resist caressing him and apparently her doing so made his cock grow bigger and harder. She felt it underneath her ass.

* * * *

Kurt's heart was pounding inside of his chest. He waited for this moment, had fought getting here for foolish reasons, and now it was time to let go and give Mercedes all of him as she gave all of her.

He lifted her up by her hips.

"Take my cock, baby. Slide down on it with this sexy, wet pussy and ride me. Things are going to get crazy," he told her.

She swallowed hard as she did what he said and then she sat on top of him, his cock in her cunt and her palms against his chest. She looked scared, unsure, and he cupped her cheeks. She was delicate, precious, and he would never allow any harm to come to her. That protective feeling filled his gut.

"What's wrong?"

"I don't know what to do," she said and shyly looked down as she lifted up and then sunk back down.

"You're doing it. Just like that. Get used to my cock being inside of you and then just follow the sensations. Rock those hips. Fuck me hard, Mercedes, like you own me," he said to her.

That seemed to do the trick because she began to set a nice steady pace and as she mastered the general technique she went faster.

He could feel his cock harden and knew it wouldn't be long before he came.

"Watching my brothers fuck you for the first time was incredible, baby."

"I'm glad I waited," she gasped as he thrust upward when she thrust down.

"That it was the three of you," she said and he thrust upward again. Then he felt her tense so he pulled her down for a kiss, knowing that Taylor was behind her with the tube of lube.

In and out she rode him faster as Taylor whispered to her and Warner washed up in the bathroom. He returned, cock in hand and ready for her mouth.

"We're going to take you together, Mercedes. Just relax those muscles and you'll be just fine. We don't want to hurt you, so you tell us if it hurts and if you need us to stop," Taylor told her and then he must have applied some of the lube to her anus because she gasped and then thrust back.

"That's it. You like my fingers in your ass you're going to love my cock," Taylor said. His words made Mercedes moan. They also made Kurt's cock grow thicker.

"Ease her up. I've got something for her," Warner said and he appeared by her side, his cock in hand.

"You ready to taste me?" he asked her and she nodded her head.

Warner gently pulled her face toward his cock and then she opened for him and began to lick and suck him.

Kurt thrust upward as Taylor pulled out his fingers and replaced them with his cock.

Mercedes moaned and grunted as she sucked on Warner's cock. Kurt thrust upward faster and Taylor pushed his cock all the way inside of her. It was wild and so intense he felt himself begin to come no matter how hard he tried holding back.

Kurt came first and then Warner. Mercedes licked Warner clean and then Warner kissed her. But he had to release his hold on her as Taylor gripped Mercedes's hips and thrust into her ass four more times as he came. He shook and then gasped for breath before kissing her spine and then easing out of her ass.

Kurt felt Mercedes collapse against his chest. He pulled from her pussy, caressed along her back, and then held her tight until she felt limp and motionless in his arms.

Warner caressed her hair from her cheeks.

"Is she sleeping?" Kurt asked as Taylor washed his cock with the washcloth and then stepped into his boxers.

He had another one for Mercedes.

"Sleeping I think."

Kurt ran his hands up and down her curves. He thought about this moment, these sensations for so long, they almost seemed unreal.

"She's finally ours," he whispered, placing a possessive hand over her bare ass.

"She sure is," Taylor said and caressed her hair.

Warner stared at her as he sat on the side of the bed next to them.

"She's in danger, and it's our job to ensure they never find her or try to take her again."

Kurt scrunched his eyes together.

"What have you learned? You know something?" Taylor asked and Kurt felt his chest tighten and his gut clench with worry. He thought about the bidding war and the pictures online. Warner explained to Taylor.

"Are you fucking kidding me? Over a million dollars? There'll be fucking psychos looking for her. What do we do? How do we protect her?" Taylor asked.

"We do what we do best. Protect what's ours. Get everyone on board and on guard. She's our woman. No one is going to lay a hand on her or hurt her ever again," Warner stated firmly.

Chapter 7

"What do you have, Pinto? Please tell me something that will make our buddies Taylor, Warner, and Kurt a little happier," Gemini asked as he looked toward Pinto. Pinto had been typing away on the computer after getting a hit with a contact to special order a woman of his choice for the right place in South Carolina.

"Bingo! I think I have a name and a company," Pinto said aloud.

"Fantastic. Slick, Breaker, you ready to start snooping?"

"We're ready, Gemini. I'm going to love when we get our hands on these assholes. It's going to be fun," Breaker said.

"Okay, here we go. The company is listed as R.J. S. National. The name associated with this company as far as I could find out is a Randall Syvretson. I am sending Breaker the pages now," Slick said and hit send.

Breaker sat forward in his seat and started typing away.

"Well?" Gemini pushed.

"Not such a low level operation. Security is high around a seven. I'll need a little time."

"Pinto, look up this guy Randall Syvretson. Find out everything you can on him," Gemini said.

"You got it," Pinto replied and began to work as well.

Gemini looked at his phone and saw it was Warner texting. He called him back.

"Hey, buddy, how did last night go?" he asked, knowing that Mercedes was with them and they hadn't planned on letting her out of their sight. He thought that was the best idea.

"It went well."

"You breaking down those walls she's got up so you can gain her trust?" he asked as they had talked about Warner leaving the job and no longer taking on private missions.

"I believe that is no longer a problem."

Gemini smiled. He felt that twinge of envy. He wished he and his brothers could be as close as they used to be.

"I'm happy for you and your brothers. We'll do our best to keep her safe. I have part of an update but we're still working on things."

"What do you have?" Warner asked.

"The name of the company setting up these bidding sites and the name of someone involved in the company. Not sure if he's an owner or not but his first name starts with the initials of the company name. R.J.S. International. His name is Randall Syvretson."

"Don't know the name or the company. Where is it located?"

"That's the thing—there are addresses for both Virginia and North Carolina. We're working on it."

"Wonderful. Keep me updated. I'll probably be over there in a while."

Gemini chuckled.

"Don't leave your woman, Warner. We've got this and we'll let you know right away if there's an update."

"Thanks."

* * * *

Warner rubbed his whiskers as he leaned against the bathroom counter. He was worried. Having Mercedes, taking her virginity and making love to her was amazing last night. He wanted her out of harm's way, but his gut said the danger was still prevalent.

"Warner?"

He heard her voice and looked toward the doorway. She stood there holding a shirt against the front of her.

"I can't find my clothes," she whispered.

He smirked. Taylor had hid them knowing she would probably want to get up and get ready for work, but he wanted the morning with her still.

Warner stepped closer, pulled her toward him by the shirt she held, and then pulled the shirt away. He grabbed her hips and looked her body over.

"You don't need any clothes. Not with this sexy body."

"I'll need them for work, silly," she said to him and then ran the palms of her hands up his chest.

She was so sweet, sexy, feminine, and precious that he felt protective of her. He didn't want to expose her to any more pain or fear. He wanted to keep her surrounded and that possessive feeling had him pulling her closer.

"Worry about it later. Right now, you and I are going to take a nice long shower."

He kissed her softly on the lips and then turned her around and slapped her ass.

"Warner," she scolded, reaching back to caress where he spanked her.

"With an ass like yours it's too tempting," he told her as she started the water up.

Warner let his eyes roam over Mercedes's backside as she stepped under the spray. When she raised her arms up to wet her hair, he could see the outline of her large breasts. He watched the water trickle down her spine then over the curve of her ass that stuck out just so. He grabbed a hold of her hips and pressed his cock against the crack of her ass.

He ran a palm along her hips then across one cheek. She was small compared to him that his one hand looked so large against her body.

"I love this ass. I can't wait to shove my dick in deep and make you come, calling my name," he said, using his palm to slide over her waist then to her mound. He cupped it and she moaned.

She went to lower her arms but he scolded her.

"Keep those hands on the wall. Palms down."

She did as he told her. She shivered and he kissed her shoulder.

"Good girl," he whispered then kissed her shoulder again.

"Now open for me. Widen that stance and let me feel that pussy."

He slowly stroked a finger up into her cunt and then used his other hand to pull her hips back toward him so her ass would stick out.

She rocked her hips in rhythm to his finger thrusts and then he pulled his fingers from her cunt and used the cream to press over her anus.

"Oh God, Warner, you're wild. You know just how to touch me," she said to him, feeding his ego, making his cock grow harder.

He licked her skin by her neck then put some pressure on a sensitive spot there. She lowered more and widened her stance.

"I've got something for you."

"Mmm…I wonder what it is?" she asked and he pressed the tip of his cock to her pussy from behind. She tilted forward and he pressed into her.

He tried to go slow but he couldn't. The way her ass stuck out just waiting for one of their cocks to sink into her turned him on. Then there was this part of him so set on claiming her, marking her his woman and his brothers' in hope that it would keep those men at bay. It was such a primal thought. It made no sense yet every part of him needed to do it. To release his seed into her body and to have every part of her so no one but him, Taylor, and Kurt would ever have her.

He pulled back and thrust into her pussy. He repeated the strokes slowly, penetrating deeply. She kept her hands on the wall and he could see her breasts bouncing with every deep thrust.

"You feel so fucking good, baby. So good," he said.

"More, Warner. More," she begged and he lost it. He reached up and gripped her shoulders and thrust up into her. Easing his hands along her arms and then to her hips, he pulled back on them and began to stroke faster and faster into her pussy. He lowered down a little and began to rock and thrust, trying to ease the itch, the need to mark her, claim her, until he heard her cry out his name. Then he let go. He gave her all of him. His cock, his seed, his fucking heart. All of him, and he knew he would never be the same man again. He thrust a few more times, coming inside her as the anxiety and worry turned to contentedness. Mercedes was safe, right here in his arms, where she belonged.

* * * *

"You need to stop teasing him. He's not always grumpy," Mercedes said to Taylor, giving him a look as Taylor joked about Warner's attitude. She thought he was a hard man. Intimidation oozed from him but it didn't frighten her like it had before.

She touched Warner's shoulder and gave him a sympathetic look. That earned Taylor a shake of Warner's head and a dirty look.

"He's got a piss-poor attitude and thinks he's the boss of the house."

"Me? Look at fucking Kurt," Warner replied. It was obvious that Warner wanted the attention to go away from him.

"Why are you bringing me into this? I don't say shit," Kurt said and gave a firm expression toward his brothers.

Mercedes chuckled.

Kurt was pretty damn tough. He didn't say much but he sure was big and strong. He barked words more than spoke them, but she didn't think he meant to.

Kurt's expression was straight faced. She swallowed hard. Maybe he did have a mean streak after all. Perhaps she really needed to push for answers about what Warner and Kurt do for a living.

"Let's sit and eat before it gets cold," Taylor said, placing the dish of scrambled eggs onto the table. Kurt held out a chair for her and she sat down between him and Warner. Taylor took the seat across from her.

Taylor looked at his brothers and then at her as they served her eggs and bacon before serving themselves.

"Next time I get to sit next to my woman." He pouted and then winked at her. She felt her belly tighten and she got all giddy inside. These men were so incredible. She was seeing sides of them she didn't know existed.

She took a bite of eggs and everyone was quiet. She couldn't help but to wonder about Kurt and Warner's jobs so she asked.

"What exactly do the two of you do for a living?"

She looked at Kurt who glanced at Warner and then at Taylor. Warner kept chewing and then Kurt put his fork down.

"It's not a job we can discuss with you," he said and she felt the rush of insult, sadness, maybe a bit of negativity about herself and how they saw her. Why couldn't they tell her? Was she not important enough? Did they not think of her the way she thought of them?

"We're not at liberty to discuss our jobs, what we've been involved in, and continue to be involved in, with anyone. Don't take offense to it, Mercedes," Warner said in that tone he had that was all commanding and in charge.

She lowered her eyes. "I'm not offended," she whispered and then picked her fork up and pretended like the comment didn't bother her.

Warner placed his arm over the back of her chair and caressed her hair.

"Don't be insulted or upset. Our jobs are with the government, honey. We do things that no one can know about."

"Dangerous things?" she asked, looking at Warner.

"Yes," he whispered.

She glanced at his chest and he followed her line of sight. He lifted her hand and placed her palm over the more recent scar he had.

"You have nothing to worry about. I'm not going to continue that job. My focus is on you and my brothers. All the things I've done in the past, the missions, the fighting, the surviving, are behind me.

You're my number one priority." He pressed her closer by the back of her shoulder and neck and he kissed her.

She felt so connected to these men. She worried, and her mind wondered how dangerous their jobs were and whether they killed anyone or came close to death themselves. But she didn't ask them. It would be rude and it wasn't right to ask such a question. She glanced at Kurt who stared at her.

"You still look like you have questions."

"No I don't," she said to Kurt and then took a bite of her forkful of eggs.

Kurt touched her chin and gave her that superior expression. He then raised one of his eyebrows up at her.

"What? I'm not lying."

"Honey, I can read you like a book. You're too sweet, too honest and real to hide your emotions," Kurt said to her and brushed his thumb along her chin.

"You can read me."

"I sure can. I know when you're happy and having a good day and when something excites you. I know when you're worried, and even when you're afraid."

"How can you, you hardly know me?" she asked.

"You don't believe me?" Kurt pushed and she shook her head.

He stared at her and thought about it a moment. She wondered what he was up to.

"How did you like those beautiful yellow flowers you saw at the supermarket?" he asked her.

She squinted her eyes at him.

"I loved them. When I saw them—"

"You smiled so wide, so bright you looked angelic."

She thought about his words. She processed them and then it hit her.

"You were there watching me? You got me the flowers?" she asked, her eyes welling up with tears.

"I couldn't approach you, talk to you then. I was still trying to work things out with myself, and waiting for Warner to get back from a business trip. Taylor said we needed to make a move and let you know how we felt about you. I didn't think twice."

"Oh God, Kurt, that's so beautiful of you."

She kissed him and then she hugged him tight.

She pulled back and smiled at Taylor.

"I was so fucking pissed off about those flowers. I tried hunting down your secret admirer but came up empty handed. Thanks to the big guy threatening everyone to keep his secret."

She chuckled.

"You were acting funny," she added.

"Baby, I was just wondering why you didn't buy those flowers yourself? You obviously loved them," Kurt asked her.

"Well, to be honest, after living on the streets and struggling to make ends meet and get a meal or two a day, I learned to not be foolish and to shop wisely. I only buy the things I really need. I've conditioned myself to be careful because there's always that fear that I could lose my job, get sick, get hurt where I can't work, and then I would be left with nothing."

Warner caressed her arm.

"That's going to change now, baby. You deserve the best of everything. We want to give you all the things you've ever wanted."

She smiled at Warner and reached up to touch his cheek.

She shook her head.

"I don't need a bunch of things, Warner. What I truly, honestly need is your love, your embraces, each of you so I feel protected and safe. I need to know that we're a team and that we can talk things through and learn to accept all our qualities."

"You got it, baby. It's our pleasure to watch over you, protect you, and love you," Taylor told her.

She smiled.

"Kurt, I'm glad you saw me in the supermarket and thought enough of me to want to make me smile. It means more than you know. Everything the three of you have done for me and how you've made me feel is so damn special, nothing will ever compare to it. So thank you," she said and then she reached for a piece of bacon and began to eat. They watched over her, smiling and sitting in quiet, just being content and maybe even thinking like Mercedes was. That she could get really used to this. To going to bed at night and into her three lovers' arms and then waking up in the morning having breakfast, talking, living lives together and then doing it all over again. Oh yeah, she could get real used to being their woman.

Chapter 8

"I don't know if I like this idea," Warner told Mercedes as she got out of the shower and walked into the bedroom to get dressed.

"What's there not to like? It's the Grand Opening of the addition at Spencer's. I want to be there for Marlena and the guys. Besides, you and Kurt will be there and Taylor will get there after work. Plus the other guys are around, too," she said as she dropped the towel and began to step into a pair of black thong panties.

"We'll be working and trying to run security there. I'm not comfortable not having myself, Kurt, or Taylor right next to you at all times," Warner told her as he absorbed her body and how truly sexy and beautiful she was.

She looked at him with those hazel eyes and a defiant expression she had lately. It seemed to him that his brothers had truly helped her with self-confidence. She didn't shy away more often than not and she stood her ground. He had to smile. It had been a month since the failed abduction and there were no signs of getting closer to the men responsible.

"It's not the same, having other men watch over you when you're our responsibility."

She walked closer to him and ran her palms along his dress shirt as if flattening out wrinkles.

"I love you, Warner. It's been a month. I can't live in fear or stop from participating in activities because those men could be out there looking. Then they win, and I've lost," she said to him.

He hadn't told her about the website and about the money men were bidding on her. He and his friends doing the investigation thought that men would lose interest and stop bidding, thinking it was fake, but then Slick noticed a date. Next week's date as the final night for bidding. They could already know where she was by now, and that scared him.

He held her close and kissed her deeply. He let his hand massage over her ass. An ass he'd just fucked this afternoon while she rode Kurt and sucked Taylor's cock while he was on lunch break. It was becoming a daily routine. Meet at their place for lunch then having Mercedes and maybe a quick bite afterwards.

He squeezed her to him as he released her lips.

"I love you, too. I just want you safe," he whispered into her ear.

Her delicate arms squeezed against his waist.

"I'll be fine. Let me get ready and I'll even go with you and Kurt so you're not late."

"We won't be late. We got everything all set. Tonight we're watching over the employees and making sure they took the training to heart and actually use what we taught them.

"Let's go," he told her and gave her ass a tap as he released her.

She smiled then walked over to the closet and took out a red dress. She grabbed it off the hanger, her back toward him, and he took in the sight of her body, the way her shoulders had definition, too, and then she had that great ass of hers. His cock hardened and he knew he couldn't make love to her again right now, but tonight would be a different story. She stepped into the red, slim-fitting dress that had an open back that fell short of her waist. His imagination got the better of him especially when she stepped into the heels. It was a short dress that looked amazing on her body, fitting it like a glove.

She turned around, running her fingers through her hair, giving them a little shake, and he smiled.

He wasn't going to be able to focus on this job tonight. Every single guy in the place would look at her and want her. He felt angry.

"Warner, don't you like it?" she asked, her voice sounding sad and her expression filled with disappointment.

He closed the distance between them and swept her into his arms.

He cupped her breast and held her gaze. She gasped.

"Are you fucking kidding me? You look incredible. You look hot, and every fucking guy is going to want what's mine. How the hell am I going to concentrate?"

She gulped as he used his thumb to caress her nipple.

"You'll concentrate because you'll remember that I'm going home with you, Taylor, and Kurt. You're the only ones I want. I love you guys, remember?"

He felt his chest tighten and he could hardly breathe as he covered her mouth and kissed her deeply. Using his other hand, he undid his pants, pushed them down, and then pulled from her.

"I need you. Don't say no. You'll fix yourself after. I need you."

She was breathing just as rapidly as he was as she nodded her head in agreement.

She slowly turned around and he lifted her dress. She pushed down her panties and then placed her hands on the bottom of the footboard.

He suckled her neck as he thrust his fingers up into her cunt.

"I need inside of you now. I need to know you're mine and my brothers'."

"Take me, Warner. I need you, too."

She gripped the wood, he pulled her hips back, spread her thighs, and aligned his cock with her pussy. He didn't hesitate as he stroked up into her and sighed in relief.

"Nothing feels better, calms me, completes me like being inside of you."

She pressed her ass back and he sought his relief, his need to feel content and assured that she wasn't going anywhere and would always be his as he thrust into her over and over again until she cried out his name and he filled her with his seed.

"Mine. All mine, always." He wrapped his arms around her waist and held her tight as he kissed her neck and absorbed how good it felt to hold her like this and love her like this. He wished he hadn't waited so long to let down his guard and to love her like she deserved. He'd make that up to her for the rest of his life.

* * * *

"I love it. It's so big and I love the extra bar and the dance floor, too. Who did all the decorating?" Mercedes asked as she sat with her friends at a table near the bar. Monroe, Caldwell, Will, Leo, and Hank were nearby, all keeping an extra eye on Mercedes. She felt safe, though. Despite the crowds, she sensed Hank and Warner nearby, too, and every so often they would stop by and kiss her.

"Alicia actually helped to decorate and come up with the great wall art and memorabilia," Marlena informed them as she gave Alicia's arm a hug.

"That stained glass artwork behind the bar is so gorgeous and unique. Love that, too, Alicia," Adele said to her and she thanked them.

Mercedes finished her drink and then stood up.

"I need to use the ladies' room," she said.

"Oh, I'll go, too," Alicia told her and before they could get past the table, Monroe stopped them.

"Where are you going?"

"Ladies' room," Alicia replied.

He nodded his head and followed them. But as he got to the hallway, someone stopped him, asking some questions.

Mercedes sighed as they entered the bathroom.

"Are you okay?" Alicia asked.

"I guess so," she said as she opened the stall and went inside.

"You know they love you so much. Max has never seen Warner, Kurt, and Taylor act like this. In love. Seemingly happy, and he knows that it's because of you," Alicia told her from the other stall.

Mercedes exited and washed her hands then looked at her lipstick.

"I doubt it's because of me," she said and Alicia came out.

"Well his friends would know. Max would. It's his job to know about things like this."

Mercedes smiled at her.

"It's crazy, isn't it? How we all came here to Chance, met one another, became friends, and never expected to fall in love."

Alicia smiled. "It sure is. But I'm glad I took a chance on Max, Monroe, and Caldwell. Though it wasn't a smooth courting," Alicia said and smirked.

"But it worked out. I hadn't wanted to take a chance, at getting close to anyone, at opening up my heart, never mind falling in love. I could have lost that chance."

"Hey, that was a freak thing. It's in the past. You have your future with Warner, Kurt, and Taylor. Hey, when is Taylor going to get here? It's almost nine," Alicia asked.

"I don't know. Soon, I hope," Mercedes said then winked at Alicia.

Alicia hugged her arm as they exited the bathroom.

"I know exactly what you mean," Alicia said and they laughed as they headed down the hallway.

The place was crowded as they came to the main area. Alicia was ahead of her and then Mercedes felt the hand on her arm. She swung around and some big, tall guy was staring at her and then he looked at his cell phone and then back at her.

"Let go of me," she demanded and tried pulling away.

"You're her. I found you," he said and then began pulling her the other way and toward the exit.

She planted her feet and tried pulling back as she yelled, drawing attention from those around her.

He stopped and pulled her close. She was shaking.

"Over a million dollars they want for you. But I found you. You're mine." He licked his lips.

"And you're fucking hotter than your pictures. And your fucking tits are huge."

She didn't know what came over her but she smacked his face and he loosened his grip.

She wasn't going to get taken again. She didn't know what the hell was going on.

"You bitch." He scolded, gripping her upper arm so tight she nearly fell to her knees but he wouldn't let her.

"Let go."

"Get your fucking hands off of her."

The guy released her arm as she heard Warner's voice and then saw Warner punch the guy, throw him to the ground then onto his belly, and cuff him.

Kurt pulled her against his chest and led her away from the man along with Monroe, Caldwell, Will, and Hank. Leo, Max, and the others remained nearby and stopped Warner from beating the crap out of the guy.

"What the hell happened? Who was that guy?" Kurt asked her as he caressed her hair from her cheek and held her against the wall in the hallway. The others were there. She felt the tears in her eyes and then Caldwell touched her shoulder and took her hand into his.

"You're hurt," he said and Kurt's eyes darkened. She could see the veins by his neck and his eyes bulging he was so angry.

"I'm okay. I'm okay, Kurt." She hugged Kurt, wrapping her arms around his shoulders, and he hugged her tight.

* * * *

"You are going to answer my fucking questions or I'm going to start tearing you apart limb from fucking limb," Warner threated the guy who tried to take Mercedes. He had him in a chair, handcuffed in Danny's office. Max was there as well as Danny, Hank, and Monroe.

The others were with Mercedes and the women, including Taylor, who'd just arrived.

"I got rights. You can't ask me shit. I was just trying to pick her up."

"Bull fucking shit. Talk, or feel fucking pain," Warner said and then pressed his thumb into the guy's shoulder in a spot that he knew would cause massive pain.

The man cried out.

"Who the fuck are you? You work for R.J.S. National or something? I was just seeing if she was as good-looking in person as the pictures. I don't have a fucking million dollars. But fuck is she worth it."

Warner slugged him.

"Warner, you can't kill him. I can't stand here and let you do this. Let's get the information and take it from here," Max said to him.

"Sorry, Max, but this whole case just got a lot fucking worse," Warner replied.

Just then someone knocked on the door. Danny opened it and Slick, Pinto, Breaker, and Gemini were there.

"This the fucking asshole?" Gemini asked.

Warner nodded.

Pinto looked at the sheriff and the others then back at Warner.

"We are taking him in for questioning. Miami is involved," Pinto told Warner.

Warner was shocked and his expressions showed it.

"What's going on and who is Miami?" Max asked.

"Max, you have to trust me and let my friends leave with this guy. It's the only way to keep Mercedes safe and possibly save other women's lives," Warner told him.

Max held his gaze and then nodded his head.

"But I expect to be kept in the loop."

"You got it," Warner said to Max then looked at Pinto then at the guy who'd tried taking his woman.

"Pinto, get this asshole out of my face before I slit his fucking throat." Warner held the man's gaze and knew his words sunk in.

"I don't want any trouble. I made a mistake," the man said as Pinto pulled him out of the chair.

"You sure did, asshole. You just don't realize yet exactly how big of a mistake you made messing with a man like my friend here," Pinto told the man as he, Gemini, and the others exited the room.

Warner placed his hands on his hips, leaned his head back, and took a deep breath then released it. He could have lost Mercedes again tonight. This shit had to stop.

"She's okay, Warner. You and Kurt got to her, and we were all nearby and would have been able to intervene and stop him," Max said.

"I understand that, but this shit has to stop. There are things going on that you don't know, Max," Warner said to him then looked at his friends.

"You need to tell me so I understand," Max replied to him.

"Mercedes is being bid on," Warner told him.

"Bid on?" Max asked.

"These men, the ones who tried to take her, wanted her so they could sell her to the highest bidder and make money off of her. Right now the bid for her is over a million dollars."

"What in God's name?" Leo asked and Warner began to explain about the information they had so far. Jack and Danny were furious.

"What are you going to do to protect her? Anyone, someone just like this asshole, could take it upon themselves to go after her and try again," Danny asked.

"I know that. I need to get that site taken down. I need to locate this Randall asshole and those other two fucks that tried abducting her," Warner replied.

"Who is this Miami person your not-so-friendly friends mentioned and seemed to shock you?" Max asked.

"Someone with enough money, power, connections, and government power to destroy an operation like this one and get Mercedes out of trouble once and for all," Warner said.

"So that's good then, right?" Jack asked.

"Yes. But it's going to cost me," Warner said and when his friends asked him to elaborate he told them he couldn't. He'd give Miami whatever he asked for, just as long as Mercedes and his brothers were safe and they didn't have to worry about her getting taken ever again.

* * * *

"My God, baby," Taylor said then pulled her into his arms and hugged her tight.

He had arrived when Kurt and Max were going over what happened to her and how some guy tried taking her. He couldn't believe what the guys said. He'd hunted her down and probably from the site men were bidding for her on. Mercedes was pissed off. He could tell. He was pissed off, too. Kurt and Warner had never mentioned the website or how serious this matter was.

"I'm okay, Taylor. I just can't believe what I'm hearing. That there's a website with my pictures on it and men are bidding on me." The tears rolled down her cheeks and she shivered.

Kurt placed his hand on her shoulder.

"Don't think about that. Our friends are taking care of it. We're going to keep you safe," Kurt told her.

"For how long? Forever? There are pictures of me in God knows what on the internet. You can't take those back. No one can delete them." She raised her voice and stood up.

"I'll let the four of you talk. I had some cruisers go by and check Mercedes's place out and yours and there's a police car out front of your places," Max said and then exited the room.

Taylor looked at Warner and Kurt.

"You were never going to tell me about this. Tell Mercedes about this site?"

"What for? So the two of you could worry like we've been?" Warner replied.

"Yes. Because we're in this together. We're brothers. Mercedes is our woman and I have a right to know everything you two do," Taylor told them.

"Don't fight. Don't let them do this to us," Mercedes said and then stood up crossing her arms in front of her chest. She took a few steps away from them.

"Mercedes, it had to be like this. We didn't want to scare you more and make you feel like you couldn't leave the house or enjoy being with your friends," Kurt told her.

She turned to look that them. "Well that's great, but I could have caused Alicia to get hurt. What if the guy had a weapon? What if you guys didn't see him grabbing me? What if he hurt you?"

"He didn't. He's a fucking loser who probably came across the site by accident, or has been watching but can't afford to bid," Kurt said to her.

"Oh God," Mercedes said and then covered her face with her hands.

"Wonderful. He won't be the only one then. Will he?" Taylor asked but they knew not to reply.

Warner stared at her, held her gaze, and then took a deep breath.

"I know you're upset. We all are, but you need to trust me. To trust us on this," Warner said to her.

She stared at him and Taylor knew she was trying to be strong. He was angry and he didn't know what to do or how to handle this. His woman's pictures were on a website and men were bidding on her, hoping to buy her. Some asshole set it all up as if Mercedes and other women were objects, merchandise to buy. It was sickening.

"I'm scared, Warner. I'm so scared," she said and tears rolled down her cheeks.

Warner pulled her into an embrace and held her. Taylor looked at Kurt who was straight faced but appeared to be biting the inside of his cheek. He would need to talk to his brothers alone later. But the thought of leaving Mercedes alone even for a moment made his heart pound inside of his chest. He couldn't lose her. He wouldn't lose her. His brothers better be ready to fill him in. No one was taking Mercedes from them. No one.

* * * *

Mercedes couldn't help but to shake. Before they even allowed her into their home, Kurt and Warner did a check over the entire house despite Max saying that some of the other deputies had already done so. Warner's phone kept buzzing, indicating he was getting texts and something was going on.

Taylor held her hand and walked her into the bedroom.

She kicked off her heels and then stared at herself in the full-length mirror in the bedroom. She loved this dress. Red always made her feel sexy and alive. She wanted to look and feel sexy for her men tonight. She clenched her eyes tight. Apparently, unbeknownst to her, someone was watching her and waiting to try and grab her. How many others were there?

She jerked and gasped the moment Taylor's hands landed on her shoulder.

"Jesus, baby. It's me. You're okay," Taylor said and then he pressed his lips to her neck.

"Let's get you undressed and into the shower. It will make you feel better."

She felt his heavy hand unzip the back of her dress. She closed her eyes as he glided his knuckles back and forth over her skin. It felt so good.

The dress fell into a puddle of material around her ankles. His hands landed on her hips and she stepped from the dress.

"I can never get enough of this body, baby. Never," Taylor told her, running his knuckles down her shoulders then caressing her ass cheeks before he slowly pressed his cock against her. She could feel the thin layer of his underwear and the nakedness of his chest and muscles. She closed her eyes, let her arms fall to her sides, and just relished in the feel of Taylor loving her.

He unclipped her bra and it fell down her arms. His thumbs glided under the material of her panties, along the thin black string, and then downward. Every inch, every caress sent waves of desire through her.

His lips touched her neck and then he suckled hard on a sensitive spot.

He wrapped his arms around her waist and pulled her close.

"I love you. I need to be inside of you."

"I love you, too. I want you inside of me," she told him.

He ran his hands down her arms over her breasts then to her mound. He cupped her pussy and she gasped.

"In the shower. Come on." He took her hand and she turned, walking with him willingly.

It wasn't long until he had the water turned on and helped her to step beneath the spray of the multiple showerheads.

"I love this shower," she whispered, closing her eyes and letting the water caress over her skin.

She thought about the man who tried taking her and about his words.

Over a million dollars they want for you. But I found you. You're mine. And you're fucking hotter than your pictures. And your fucking tits are huge.

She shivered then felt Taylor's arms wrap around her, hugging her.

"Don't be scared. It's over, and you're here with me."

She turned in his arms and stood on tiptoes as she pulled his face lower. "I need you inside of me. I need you taking his voice away and the words he said to me. Please, Taylor, make love to me please," she begged of him then kissed him.

He kissed her deeply and she got lost in the feel of his touch. His fingers found her pussy and pressed up into her. She reached down for his cock, running her hand back and forth over it, feeling it enlarge and get thicker. She cupped his balls and he moaned into her mouth.

In a flash he pulled fingers from her pussy, gripped her hips, and lifted her up and against the wall. Her back hit the tile and the waterheads cascaded over them, between them, and suddenly she felt hot, faint, needy. She reached under as he did and grabbed hold of his erection then aligned it with her cunt. She sunk down as he pressed upward and then they both exhaled in relief.

"Heaven, fucking heaven," he said.

She grabbed onto his shoulders, closed her eyes, and got lost in his strokes and the depth of which the act of making love seemed to reach.

"Mercedes. God, baby, you feel so fucking good."

"Yes, Taylor. More, harder I need you," she told him and counterthrust downward. He covered her mouth and kissed her again as he stroked faster and faster into her cunt.

She loved the feel, the friction of her breasts rubbing against his pectoral muscles with every stroke. He was her lover, her man, and she adored him. She immediately thought about Kurt and Warner and wanted them, too.

"Fuck, I'm coming. Come with me, baby," he told her and she felt her body tighten and then his strokes deepen and speed up.

"Taylor. Oh God, Taylor," she moaned as she came and Taylor grunted and thrust one more time, shooting his seed into her womb. He laid his mouth against her shoulder and neck, his breathing heavy as he recovered.

"Mine. I'll always be her for you, baby. Always."

She hugged him tight and prayed that he could do just as he said and be here for her always.

* * * *

"Are you sure? Are you absolutely fucking sure?" Warner asked Gemini over the phone.

Kurt was next to him listening on speakerphone.

"I closed down the site but not before placing a picture of her handcuffed and blindfolded, wearing panties and a bra, being led by you, smiling. We placed a huge 'Sold' sign on the page across the picture. The bids halted, the followers disappeared, and we deleted the account. Plus Slick sent a little virus to all the fuckers who were on the site, so I doubt they'll be trusting anything R.J.S. National puts up from now on."

"That's fucking awesome. God. I hope it worked and that no one will still try to take her," Kurt said.

"There's always that chance, but we'll have to wait and see. In the interim, Miami has organized a team as you requested to destroy the operation. He wants to see you in his office tomorrow," Gemini stated.

"What's this about, Warner? Who is Miami?" Kurt asked him.

"I'll take care of it, Gemini. Thanks for everything you've done. I'll talk to you tomorrow."

"I sure as shit hope so. Watch your ass. Miami has something up his sleeve."

"I hear you, and I will."

Warner disconnected the call and then leaned back in his chair. He had a lot to think about.

"So spill the beans. Who is this Miami and why are you going to see him tomorrow?" Kurt asked.

"He's one of the connections. The one who has gotten me some pretty fucked-up jobs over the years."

"You said you were finished," Kurt said, sitting forward. He glanced at his shirt and Warner knew he was probably thinking about the gunshot to his shoulder. A flesh wound that could have been the death of him.

He looked away from his brother and then back at Kurt.

"She needs to feel safe and to be safe. I, we can't do this alone. This is a bigger operation than any of us had suspected. The right people in the government are involved now and this should end."

"You're not going to see him. You don't have to. This is the government's job and not this dick who is going to hold it over your head. What is he going to do, send you on another dangerous mission?"

Warner stood up.

"Whatever he needs me to do. Mercedes is our priority."

"And if you die?" Kurt shot at him and stood up.

"You and Taylor will take good care of her and love her like we talked about."

Kurt ran his fingers through his hair. "This is fucking bullshit."

"It's the way it has to go down. If Miami finds these men and captures them, bringing justice to Mercedes and all those other women, then it will be worth it to go out one more time and pay my debt."

"And if he doesn't succeed, then what?"

"Then there's no debt to pay. Just don't tell Mercedes about this."

"And Taylor?"

"We need to talk to him. He's still upset."

"We will, or rather I will. For now on, Mercedes is never left alone. Even in this house."

* * * *

Kurt climbed into bed and locked gazes with Taylor.

"Warner is downstairs," he whispered. Taylor nodded. He eased his body out from next to Mercedes and Kurt took his place. Kurt brought Mercedes's arm over his chest and then ran his hands along her hips to her ass. He watched her sleep. She was an angel, so sweet and caring, and she didn't deserve to be scared or hurt.

He trailed a finger along her ass and down the crack. She moved and he smirked.

He stared at her breasts and lowered down to take a taste. He licked the tiny bud and then pulled gently on it. She moaned softly.

"I know you're awake. I need you," he told her and then rolled her to her back and climbed between her legs.

He eased up and she blinked her eyes open then smiled. "Kurt." She said his name in a soft purr that aroused his dick. He pressed his cock between her pussy lips and began to ease his way inside.

"Let me in, Mercedes. Give me all of you."

"Always, Kurt," she said as she ran her hands up his chest and over his shoulders. She rubbed him up and down as he began to sink his cock deeper and deeper into her pussy.

"Yes, Kurt. Yes," she said, tilting her head back, giving him full access to her body. He licked along her throat then nipped her chin.

"I love you. I love being inside of you."

"I love you, too," she said and he began to rock a little faster. He lifted her thighs higher and his mind drifted off as he stared at her large breasts swaying with every stroke of his cock. He thought about the man that touched her, grabbed her, and hurt her arm, leaving bruises. He stroked even faster and she moaned and gripped his arms tight as he fucked her, trying to destroy the memories of the incident and know for certain that Mercedes was right here with him, in his house with his brothers, too.

"Oh God. Oh!" she exclaimed as she shook and came. He lost his focus and he couldn't hold back. She drove him wild. Her body, the depth of the love he had for Mercedes, sent him over the edge and into his climax. He grunted and then growled as he came, then hugged her to him before rolling to the side and gently pressing her head to the crook of his neck.

"This is where you belong. Always." He kissed her forehead and she closed her eyes and cuddled close.

They had to keep her safe. They had to.

* * * *

"I understand why you didn't fill me in, but considering I'm law enforcement I think it's pretty fucked up. But I forgive you. You and Kurt thought you were doing the right thing," Taylor said as he leaned back in the chair.

"There's more. But this stays between you, me, and Kurt, okay?"

Taylor nodded his head.

"Without getting into too many details or dodging your questions you're going to have, I may need to leave for a few days."

Taylor sat forward in his seat.

"Leave? Where? Why?"

Warner exhaled.

"I thought you weren't going to do anymore fucking government missions. What about Mercedes? And now, when all this shit is going on?"

"The guy that my friends mentioned was helping us, the one I said I would owe a favor to if he helped resolve this situation and catch the men trying to take Mercedes?"

"Yeah?"

"I'll owe him whatever he asks. I'm assuming it will involve a secret job, but I don't know. I'll do whatever is necessary to keep Mercedes safe. I'll do it for her."

"But how can you make this type of deal with the man without discussing things first? Have you been working with him all along?"

"No. I'm meeting him tomorrow."

"I don't like this. What if something happens to you, then what?"

"You and Kurt take care of Mercedes and love her."

"No. That's not what we talked about and what we wanted to have together in sharing her. It isn't right, and when Mercedes finds out she's going to flip. You won't be able to leave her."

"She isn't going to find out because no one is going to tell her," Warner said firmly.

"Then you'll lose the trust you gained."

"I'll gain it back after I know she's safe and out of harm's way. I have no choice. Miami has already helped Gemini and the others take down the website and the bidding war."

Warner explained what went down and Taylor was silent.

"I've never asked you or Kurt exactly what you do, what your jobs are when you disappeared for weeks or months at a time."

"Then don't ask now. Let me take care of our family. You and Kurt watch over Mercedes while I'm gone."

Taylor nodded his head.

"Nothing better go wrong, or I'm going to be seriously pissed off at you."

Warner nodded his head.

"I'll do anything for Mercedes. I'd give my life if necessary."

"So would Kurt and I. Let's hope it doesn't come to that."

Chapter 9

"I don't understand how this happened. Who are these men?" Jeff asked Randall over the phone.

"Obviously you underestimated them," Randall replied and paced his office. This was bad. Really, really bad because the bosses knew about Mercedes and the bidding war. They were demanding to know who took her and where the money was.

"We have bigger problems. The bosses heard about the sale," Randall told Jeff.

"So tell them what happened. Tell them someone hacked into the computer system but that Mercedes is still available. But off-line. We know our big money buyers well. In a situation like this we should contact someone overseas. Get her out of the country. Call in someone who can get into that small town and grab her right out from underneath that deputy and his buddy."

"You're not getting this. No one will touch this situation at this point. I have no choice but to beg for forgiveness for fucking this up."

"Don't do that, Randall. Leave it to Damien and I. We'll get her even if we have to kill the deputy and his buddy. We'll get her."

Randall disconnected the call. He was pissed off. The company had expanded in leaps and bounds. He was involved in so many business deals right now he wondered if he should just dump the selling of women. It was a dirty business, and with the Ukrainians taking over, he should sell out now while he was ahead.

He thought about and decided to wait out Jeff and Damien. Selling Mercedes for over a million dollars would be the last sale. The others could be passed along with the business. He would make the call. His bosses had an interest in taking over. He would give them a good price for the contacts and the employees, and he would also get the money from the sale of Mercedes to the highest bidder. This would work. It had to.

* * * *

Mercedes gasped and sat up in bed. She was having another nightmare. This time instead of it being Jeff or Damien it was the same man from Spencer's trying to take her.

"Are you okay?" Warner asked her as her eyes adjusted to the darkness.

She looked to the left, feeling the hand caress her hip. Kurt was there.

"Yes," she whispered then noticed that Warner was still wearing his dress pants. He wasn't wearing a shirt, and Taylor was asleep in the recliner near the bed.

She looked at the clock. It was four thirty.

"You haven't come to bed yet?" she asked Warner as she sat up a little higher, taking the sheet to hold up against her bare chest.

He looked down at the floor as he sat on the side of the bed. His head was in his hands then he ran his fingers over his head to his neck and moved like he was stiff and sore, or maybe stressed. He was upset about tonight. He felt responsible.

Mercedes sat up then moved closer to Warner as she tucked her knees under her bottom and began to massage his shoulders. She worked his muscles, feeling how tense he was but also having difficulty because his muscles were so big and defined.

"I would do anything for you, Mercedes. You know that, right?" he asked and looked up, turning his head to the side so she could see him.

"I know," she whispered and kissed his shoulder and ran her palms up and down his back. "And I would do anything for you, Kurt, and Taylor," she added then continued to kiss his skin before she hugged him.

Warner turned in her embrace and she slid to the side then knelt up and kissed him. She tasted his lips, took her time to explore them while he allowed her to. She pressed her tongue deeply into his mouth and he pulled on it, drawing her in deeper and taking that control all three of her men had to have.

She ran her hands along his torso and he turned then scooped her up as if she weighed nothing at all and placed her on his lap straddling his waist. She was totally naked and he gripped her hips and gave them a jerk. "I love you, and I love this body." Warner was breathing differently, almost as if he were shaking as he said the words. She locked gazes with him as she held onto his shoulders. He licked her nipple, lifting her hips higher so he could feast on her right breast and then her left. He held her still as she knelt up and then he maneuvered a finger up into her pussy.

"Oh," she moaned softly.

"You're wet," he whispered back.

"You do it to me," she replied and he took a deep breath, held her gaze with his firm one, and then continued to stroke her pussy while he feasted on her breast. Her entire body tightened and hummed with need for more of him.

"Warner, please," she panted. He pressed against her clit, massaged her pussy lips, and rubbed them, causing tiny vibrations to build up in her core. She felt more cream release and she reached down and unzipped his pants.

"Oh no. I have another idea," he told her then removed his fingers and lifted her up. He placed her feet down on the rug, and then turned her around and she spotted Kurt.

"On all fours now. Legs spread wide," he said and made quick work of his fingers taking off his pants the rest of the way.

She felt his hands on her ass then once again fingers stroked her pussy.

Kurt watched her.

"She's so beautiful," Kurt said aloud.

"She sure is and we're very lucky to have her as our woman," Warner replied then pulled his fingers from her pussy and replaced them with his cock. She barely sensed the tip of his cock when suddenly he began to push completely into her. She cried out from the thick, hard size of his cock and gripped the comforter.

Smack.

"This ass is ours. This body is ours and no one else's," he said, shocking her that he spanked her ass.

She pressed her ass back and he smacked it again and again as he pumped his hips, rocking her forward.

Kurt knelt up and gripped her cheeks.

"I need that sexy mouth. You got my cock so hard, Mercedes. I can see how turned on you are at getting spanked."

"Oh God," she moaned.

Smack.

"Oh!" she cried out.

Kurt brought his cock to her lips and she opened immediately. These men made her wild. They made her want things and need things she never knew existed. The power of their bond, this relationship was never ending and life altering. She sucked deeper, making Kurt moan and then grab a fistful of her hair.

"Holy fuck that mouth. Jesus, Mercedes, that feels incredible," Kurt told her.

"She's a quick learner," Taylor said, joining them.

Warner was thrusting faster and faster. His hold on her hips was so firm as his fingers dug into her flesh that she cried out, feeling aroused at his possessiveness.

"Don't you come yet. You come when all three of us are inside of you." Warner grunted and then pumped his hips a little slower, torturing her.

"Ready?" Kurt asked and Taylor must have said yes but she was so lost in the sensations and in trying to keep up with the thrusts from Warner and Kurt that she hadn't heard.

Then Kurt eased his cock from her mouth and Taylor slid under her as Warner lifted her from around the waist. It all turned her on. How her men worked in sync with one another and knew how they wanted to make love to her.

In a flash Warner pulled from her pussy and Taylor took over. She sunk down onto his cock as he gripped her hips and rocked upward. Then Kurt pulled her down so she could continue to suck his cock, but she sensed Warner moving away.

"He's not far. Just grabbing the lube," Kurt told her and she felt aroused and her anus tightened just thinking about what was coming.

A moment later as she sucked Kurt and Taylor thrust upward into her pussy, Warner pressed the lube to her anus and worked it in. In and out he thrust two fingers, scissoring them, getting her ass ready for his cock.

Smack.

She moaned and Kurt grunted.

"Get in her ass before I come," he complained.

Then she felt Warner's fingers pull out and then his cock press in. He worked it slowly as not to hurt her and she thrust backward.

Smack.

"Slow down and ease up those muscles."

She felt the *pop* as he eased his cock fully into her ass. He gripped her tighter and then grunted. They all worked their cocks into her together and she rocked and swayed between them. She wanted to come. She was there. Kurt thrust into her mouth and came. She swallowed his essence and then licked him clean.

Warner and Taylor were moving rapidly and Warner was calling her name when she begged to come.

"Please let me come. Please," she cried out.

"Hold on. Just a little more, baby," Warner ordered and then Taylor came.

"Now, Mercedes. Come now," Warner commanded as he thrust his cock deep into her ass then pulled on her nipples. She cried out and she rocked her hips and swayed back and forth. Warner followed and then roared before he hugged her tight.

"Know that I will always love you and that you're a part of me no matter what," Warner said to her and she felt nervous and unsure about his comment. She wondered why he would say such a thing, but then they began to take care of her. Taylor eased out of her pussy and Kurt walked to the bathroom and got a washcloth and began to clean her up. Warner kissed her all over her body then smiled.

"Go to sleep, baby. We'll be right here watching over you."

She closed her eyes and cuddled next to Kurt and Taylor as she watched Warner and absorbed him caressing her skin. This was heaven, and she wasn't going to let anything get in the way of their happiness. Nothing. No one.

* * * *

"Are you sure about this?" Kurt asked Mercedes.

"Yes. I need to go to work. What am I going to do? Sit around here and wait for someone else to try and take me?" she asked.

Kurt got angry. He didn't want to think about that possibility. He also didn't want to scare her or let on to what was happening. How Warner was going to leave them for God knew how long. He didn't want his brother sacrificing himself and putting himself in danger like this. There had to be another way. Perhaps a break in the case, an arrest, something had to give.

"Don't say that. With the website taken down and made to look like you've been sold, no one else should come looking for you."

She gave him a sideways look, raising one of her eyebrows up at him.

"And you believe that?" she replied sarcastically. She turned around to head out of the room. Kurt grabbed her hand and pulled her into his arms.

He placed his hand over her ass, hoisting her up against his chest.

"I don't know which one of you I like better. The quiet, nonconfrontational Mercedes, or this new sassy, speak-her-mind Mercedes."

She took a deep breath and exhaled.

"They're one in the same. Besides, it's you and your brothers' faults for bringing it out in me."

"Our faults?" he asked, caressing a finger down the crack of her ass, earning him a heated gaze and her delicate fingers dug into his arms.

"Yes, your faults." She ran her hands up and down his arms and he lifted her one thigh up and against him as he used his other hand to maneuver under her skirt. He trailed his thumb along the thin string of her panties, massaging and manipulating her ass cheek, then stroking a finger against her puckered hole.

Her face turned a nice shade of pink and he squinted at her.

"You're our responsibility. We fight your battles, we protect you so you can always be that sweet, quiet, sexy Mercedes who thinks the world is an amazing place and that strangers are just new friends you haven't had the chance to meet yet."

"You make me sound gullible and easily manipulated," she scolded.

"Oh no, not at all gullible." He kissed her neck and suckled against her skin. He pressed his fingers lower and found her pussy lips.

He stroked a digit up into her pussy and she began to rock her hips, press her breasts against his chest, and then moan softly as he kissed along her throat.

"Wouldn't you rather stay home with me this morning and play? I've got some things I'd like to show you."

"Things?" she whispered as he pumped his fingers a little faster, feeling her cream drip from her cunt.

"Oh yeah, rope, some handcuffs maybe, and a little leather whip. That way I can tie you up and have my wicked way with you." He suckled her neck harder right against a sensitive spot and she thrust her hips faster.

"Sounds like fun. But can I trust you to not leave me lying on your bed, tied up and naked and all alone?" she asked.

He pulled his fingers from her pussy, lifted her up, and placed her onto the table in the kitchen.

"Baby, there's no way I would leave you. Just thinking about you naked, tied up to my bed, vulnerable and handing all control over me has me so riled up, I wouldn't be able to leave you. You'll be begging for mercy and I'll be fucking this mouth," he said and kissed her.

"This pussy," he said and pressed his thumbs over her mound then lowered her to her back as he undid his pants and shoved them down.

"And fucking this ass, so hard, so deeply, you won't know what's happening. You'll feel sedated." He pressed a finger over her cunt, using her cream to wet his digit and then he pressed it against her anus.

"Oh God, Kurt. You're so crazy and wild. I don't know why I'm so turned on right now. I don't know if I could let you tie me down and have all that control over me."

He pulled his finger from her anus and then pressed his cock to her cunt. He slowly pushed into her.

"Oh, you'll let me. In fact right after I make love to you this morning, I'm grabbing that stuff and we're heading to my bedroom." He thrust into her fully and she cried out, coming around his cock and he couldn't help but to smile. He thrust and thrust faster and faster as he gripped her thighs and brought them higher against his waist.

"Kurt! Oh God, Kurt." She moaned and shook again. He was relentless with his strokes and the sight of her breasts pouring from her blouse and her skirt up around her waist, and the sound of flesh slapping against flesh sent him over the edge. "Mine. You drive me fucking wild, baby. Wild." He roared and then came.

As he shook, he thrust a few more times, teeth clenched, body tight, and his mind thinking about the next step. He manipulated her all right. And now she would be safe in his arms, in his bed for another day and night. Hopefully that would help him deal with the constant bad feeling in his gut that just couldn't seem to go away.

"What do we have here?" Taylor asked as he walked into the kitchen in full uniform. Hank watched Mercedes's eyes light up and then roam over his brother's body. He chuckled.

Hank helped Mercedes to sit up as she fixed her blouse.

He cupped her cheek and she looked at him with passion in her eyes that melted his heart and made him love her even more.

"We were just making plans for today. My bed, some rope, handcuffs, and that little black whip I have that's sure to get her pussy and ass ready for cock all day long." He kissed her lips and when he released them she looked drugged.

"Handcuffs? That's my line, bro," Taylor said and tapped his handcuffs that sat on his waist before he reached over, cupped Mercedes's cheek, and kissed her.

When Taylor released her lips he smiled.

"Save some energy for when I stop by at lunchtime. I'll be thinking about all the ways I can restrain you and fuck you in my forty-five minute break." He traced her nipple with his finger and she gulped.

"I need to get going. I'll let Max know she's taking the day." He winked and then Mercedes looked at him and gave his chest a slap.

"You're a piece of work. Easily manipulated?" she asked and he chuckled.

"Don't blame your weakness on me. Apparently you have an appetite for being naughty and a secret desire to be restrained during sex, and I'm the man to help you through your first of many, many times," he said, pulling her by her thighs against his waist before he cupped her cheeks and kissed her deeply.

He loved her so very much. Today was going to be a very interesting day and he was now looking forward to it.

* * * *

Warner drove the Camaro out of town. He was going to meet Miami at a secret location. He was glad that he could slip out of the house while his brother gave full attention to Mercedes. He couldn't help but smile as he thought about what he overheard. Seems Mercedes had a secret desire of being restrained during sex. That would be his happy thought today and how he would participate in that activity once he got home later. But for now his focus was on getting into his mercenary state of mind and dealing with Miami. What would the bastard ask for? How could he ensure Mercedes's safety? He needed facts, definites, and not empty promises. He wanted to end this old life and move on with a new one with Mercedes and his brothers. But how could he, when he had this feeling that whatever Miami asked for, it would risk Warner's life and that no longer fed the adrenaline rush like years before. He wasn't in the right frame of mind. There wouldn't be any motivation and that was when the risk of getting killed increased.

Warner found the place immediately and saw the black SUV with tinted windows parked alongside the building. There was a guard there. A guy standing in regular clothes but armed and ready.

He parked the car and got out and headed toward the man. He didn't recognize him. Warner had been out of the loop and not dealt with Miami's security for quite some time. He sized the guy up and knew he could take him if necessary. The guy nodded his head and looked a little worried. Perhaps he knew Warner's reputation after all?

"I need to search you for weapons."

"You're not searching shit. I am carrying. That's my given right, and, we're on the same team. Work for the same government, so cut the bullshit," he said firmly. The guy placed his hand against his ear. Obviously others were listening in and Warner got more tense and on guard.

"Miami said it's fine," the guy told him then opened the door. Warner stepped inside.

It was an old place, run-down and unoccupied by a business. He saw Miami sitting at a table, the only clean one in the place. They locked gazes.

"It's been a while, Warner. You look good."

"As do you, Miami," he said and Miami stood up and shook his hand then brought him in for a hug. It made Warner tense. There was a time, years ago, when they were in training together that he thought of Miami as a friend. But in this case, Miami had grown into a powerful government resource. He also had the ability and control to end a person's life if he chose to.

They sat down and Miami tapped his fingers on a file that sat on the table.

"How is your girlfriend? Safe and sound and with your brothers?" he asked.

Warner nodded.

"That's good. I'm happy for you. She's quite a knockout. Something tells me this won't be the last time you and your brothers have to fight to keep other men away from her. But the real problem is this organization interested in finding her now."

"You don't think shutting down the website and saying she was sold already would keep them at bay?" Warner asked.

Miami shook his head. His dark black eyes held Warner's and Warner could see the bits of gray in Miami's black hair. He also wasn't doing as good shape as years ago. Desk jobs, verbal commands, and nonfrontline action tend to soften a man in a lot of ways. Warner would never get like that. Training and being prepared meant too much to him.

"That company your friends and you figured out were the culprits behind this business of abducting and selling women for money, is not so minor. Not sure if you know, but a man by the name of Nicolai Vollup, a Ukrainian organized crime boss has been taking control of many businesses like this one for the past year. In doing so, he has caused a bit of friction with certain individuals our government provides protection for because of their connections and power."

"Dirty, secret business as usual even with organized crime bosses? Yeah, I get that," Warner said. Miami nodded.

"So you understand that there is more at stake here than saving your girlfriend and even the other women still for sale by this Randall individual?"

"Not really because the other shit doesn't matter to me. I just want Mercedes safe and sound. I want this whole bidding thing on her to disappear and for no other jackasses obsessed with her pictures online to show up thinking they can have her. That's why I'm here. You said you can stop it. So tell me how you guarantee to do that and then what you want in return."

Miami leaned back and slowly pushed the file toward Warner.

"This problem is one in the same. I can ensure Mercedes is safe. I have the location of the two men that tried to abduct her as well as the location of Randall who is about ready to sell off his little women selling business to Nicolai Vollup for a hefty sum of money."

Warner sat forward. "So you're going to give me all that information so I can get them arrested?"

He tapped the file. "Everything is in here along with instructions on an upcoming operation you'll find interesting. You'll see that your part in this as I ask is necessary and the only way to repay me for my abilities to get this to you in a timely manner."

"What do I have to do? What's the bottom line?" Warner asked.

Miami held his gaze.

"I need Nicolai Vollup dead."

* * * *

Taylor stood in Max's office as Warner spoke with Max and him over the speakerphone.

"What do you need us to do?" Max asked.

"Nothing," Warner replied and Taylor could hear the strain in his brother's voice. Something was wrong. He had that meeting with Miami. That's how he got all this information. But what had Miami asked for in return?

"What do you mean nothing?" Max asked.

"Gemini and the others, along with some representatives from the government, are taking care of all of it. Jeff and Damien, the two men who tried abducting Mercedes the first time, should be under arrest at this moment. Randall will be in custody in no time and his company R.J.S. National will be destroyed as well."

"Where are you now? Are you heading to our place to tell Kurt and Mercedes?"

Warner was quiet and Taylor didn't like that. He looked at Max who held his gaze with a knowing grim expression.

"Warner?"

"Taylor, I need you, Kurt, Max, and the others to watch over Mercedes while I'm gone."

"Gone? Where? What are you talking about, you're leaving?"

"I need to take care of something to ensure that Mercedes and you and Kurt are safe so that we can move on with our lives and a future with Mercedes."

"Warner, you can't just leave without seeing Mercedes and explaining things to Kurt and I," Taylor said to him.

"Taylor, it has to be like this. Don't make it harder. I need to focus."

"Well what about us? What will Mercedes do if something happens to you?"

"Nothing is going to happen. I don't plan on getting killed. Just take care of her and let me handle this."

"I don't know if I can. Not now. Things are different," Taylor said and glanced at Max. He felt awkward talking like this in front of him but Max was like another brother to all of them. They had been friends for years.

"Please, Taylor. Take care of Mercedes and let me handle this."

"Fine, but if anything happens to you, I'll fucking beat the crap out of you."

Warner chuckled.

"Never happen. I'll try to get back as quickly as I can."

"You'd better. Be safe, Warner."

"Yes, be safe, buddy," Max added then Warner disconnected the call.

Taylor ran his fingers through his hair.

"He'll be fine. He's one tough bastard, always has been," Max said to Taylor.

"I've had this bad feeling in my gut for weeks now. I don't like it. I'm not certain."

"Taylor, this is what your brother does. If he says he needs to do this than he needs to. Stay positive and take care of Mercedes."

Taylor nodded his head then looked at the clock. He had another thirty minutes before lunch.

"Leave now. Take the full hour and go see her and Kurt. It will make you feel better," Max told him and smirked.

"Thanks, Max. For understanding, for being such a good friend, for everything."

Max nodded and then Taylor headed out of the department and straight for home.

* * * *

"Oh God, Kurt, that tickles," Mercedes said as she lay on her belly, her hands tied with rope on long leads attached to the posts of the bed. Kurt was using some sort of leather contraption like a feather duster but instead of feathers they were thin strips of leather. She could smell them and the feel of them slapping against her ass cheeks was making her feel aroused and horny.

She wiggled her hips and he lifted her hips higher.

"Your ass is so fucking perfect. I don't know if I'm going to fuck it first, or fuck this pussy," he said and slapped her pussy from underneath with the leather duster.

"Do it. I don't care, you're making me crazy."

"Hot damn, now this is something to come home to." She heard Taylor's voice and gasped as cream dripped from her cunt. She was half embarrassed by being caught and not even hearing Taylor come into the house, and half turned on because obviously Kurt had heard his brother and apparently she wanted her men to see her like this.

Taylor's palm glided along her ass cheeks and up her spine.

"You look so fucking sexy," he said and leaned down and kissed her lips. As he plunged his tongue into her mouth he cupped her breasts.

"Now I don't have to choose. Taylor can help me fill you with cock. Is that what you want?"

"Yes. Yes, now do it," she panted.

"Sweet Jesus you got her begging for it," Taylor said and quickly took off his clothes. He was on the bed in a flash. She saw his cock and opened her mouth just as Kurt spanked her with the duster.

"Oh God," she got out as Taylor stroked his cock into her mouth.

"Fuck yeah," Taylor said and Kurt's hands massaged her ass then pressed a finger to her anus.

She pushed back, needing it. She craved his cock, their cocks to penetrate her ass and her pussy and eliminate this hunger and need so deep in her core she was shaking. She wanted to come, to find that release they always brought her and she wanted it now.

She felt Kurt pull back and then Taylor grabbed her hair and slowly pumped into her mouth.

Behind her the bed dipped and then she felt the cool liquid to her ass. She sucked faster, wanting, needing to come and feeling overwhelmed with desire.

Kurt's fingers slid right into her ass as he pumped three times then pulled them out. She moaned in annoyance.

Smack.

That earned her a smack and then a nibble to each ass cheek as her pussy clenched some more.

She tried moving her hands but couldn't. The feel of the rope loose around her wrists tugged at her every time. She couldn't touch Taylor or reach back and touch Kurt. They had her restrained and as she felt her heart race faster, Kurt thrust into her ass in one smooth stroke.

She thrust back and forth until Taylor pulled from her mouth. Her pussy swelled with need and she couldn't finger herself or even reach her pussy.

She growled out.

"What's wrong, baby?" Taylor asked, knowingly, as his eyes zeroed in on hers, reading them.

"Please," she begged.

"You need my cock somewhere else?" he asked and she nodded her head as Kurt fucked her ass good and hard.

"Tell me where?" Taylor pushed, easing under her and brushing over her pussy lips, teasing her.

"Please, Taylor. Please."

Smack.

"Oh," she gasped as Kurt smacked her ass and made the sensations intensify.

"Tell him," Kurt said.

"My pussy. I need your cock in my pussy. Now!" she added as she exhaled in annoyance.

Taylor smiled and Kurt shoved balls deep into her ass, lifting her hips.

"Why didn't you just say so?" Taylor said. He slid underneath her and the ropes and in a flash she felt the tip of his cock at her pussy and she sunk down hard. All three of them moaned and that was it. Taylor and Kurt fucked her relentlessly until she came several times and felt like a sedated, limp noodle.

As they grunted and thrust then finally came inside of her she collapsed against Taylor's chest.

She moaned from the pulling on the ropes.

"Slow down, baby. We've got you," Kurt said, slipping out of her and then undoing the ropes. He kissed her right wrist and made sure she wasn't marked and Taylor kissed her left wrist and then brought her arms up over his shoulders as he hugged her tight.

"I love you, baby. Always." And he kissed her.

* * * *

"Where the hell is he? Why aren't you telling me? I want to know," Mercedes demanded.

Taylor looked at Kurt.

"He needed to take care of something. He'll be gone for a few days, maybe longer."

"What? He didn't even tell me or say good-bye or nothing," she said, sounding very sad.

Kurt pulled her closer to him as he sat on the edge of the bed. She was standing between his legs, wearing Kurt's shirt and nothing else.

Kurt moved his palms up her ass to her lower back and then back down again.

"Baby, look at me," Kurt said to her. He could see the tears in her eyes. The concern.

"He's coming back. This was important."

"Does it have to do with the men who tried taking me? Is he taking matters into his own hands?"

Kurt took a deep breath and released it.

"You need to accept what Taylor and I are telling you and not to ask any questions."

"But—"

He raised both eyelids.

"No buts. If Warner and I had to continue doing what we've done as a profession for all these years, then you would need to accept that and not ask questions."

She stared at him and licked her lower lip before speaking.

"But you're not doing that anymore. Warner told me he was done and that the last job he had he came close to getting hurt. I don't want him to get hurt because of me."

He ran his hands up her thighs to her ass and then her hips. He pulled her closer as she gripped his shoulders.

"You're our woman and we're here to protect you. Please, understand that when Warner returns it's his decision of whether to let you know where he was and what he was doing. We need you to respect his wishes. He doesn't want you worrying. He wants you safe, just as Taylor and I do."

She looked at Taylor and Kurt could see she wasn't buying any of this and she was truly hurt, worried, and upset with them and Warner.

"Well, you're not leaving me any choice but to accept this. But for the record, it sucks."

Kurt was surprised by her reply as he smirked and then slowly lifted her shirt. "There's a lot to be said for sucking," he teased then licked her nipple before sucking it into his mouth. He fell back, taking her with him, landing on the bed and locking gazes with her.

"Very funny, Kurt," she told him and he rolled her to her back and rocked his hips against her naked mound.

"Someone feeling a little sassy?" he asked and Taylor chuckled.

"I'll leave you to give her a nice spanking for her sassiness. Some of us have to get back to work," Taylor said and he ran his hand along her ass as he bent and kissed her. Before he stood up, he smacked Mercedes's ass. The sound echoed through the room.

"Taylor!" she reprimanded and Kurt heard his brother laughing as he left the room.

"Now, where were we?" Kurt asked her as he caressed her backside.

She held his expression with a stern one.

"Oh no you don't, baby. You are not getting away with that."

He quickly sat up, using his strong core muscles, and flipped her around on his lap, placing her over it on her belly and then began to spank her ass. She wiggled and laughed, begging him for mercy until he stroked a finger up into her cunt. She didn't move until he stroked a few more times then felt her hips rocking downward against his finger.

"Damn, baby, I think you're going to be my new full-time job."

He stroked faster, pulled his fingers out of her pussy, smacked her butt a few times, and then stroked her again and again until she cried out her release. He smiled wide. She was perfect for him and for his brothers. He prayed that Warner came back safely. They weren't complete unless the four of them were together and safe, here in Chance.

Chapter 10

"Dom, I appreciate you meeting me on such short notice," Warner said to the Russian as they shook hands and he took a seat in front of Dom's desk.

"I haven't heard from you in years, and in a matter of a month, your name has popped up several times."

Warner felt that bit of fear that things weren't working in his favor with this. He didn't trust Miami, but Miami had more power and control than he did. What Warner needed to do was let this Russian take out Nicolai so Warner wouldn't have to get his hands dirty.

"Well you can't believe everything you hear," Warner replied, holding the Russian's gaze.

"I don't know, my friend. Miguel was quite the powerful drug lord."

"Miguel?" Warner replied, playing dumb. Dom chuckled.

"I get it. No need to count our kills. So tell me why you need to meet with me. I doubt you want to take up my offer of joining my team." Dom raised one of his eyebrows at Warner in challenge.

"Not for me. In fact, after this last situation gets resolved I plan on retiring."

"Retiring? You? Tell me it isn't so."

Warner smirked.

"Ahh, who is she?"

Warner felt on the defensive and instantly wanted to protect Mercedes from everyone and everything.

"Okay. I get it. Good for you. Now, talk to me."

Warner began to explain about the business of selling abducted women.

"You mean R.J.S. International?" he asked, and Warner felt like cheering. He had a feeling Dom would know them.

"You know of them?"

"I have associates who are in the process of buying shares."

"You mean buying out the company?"

Dom held his gaze.

"What is going on?"

"Your buddies are about to get screwed and screw you over big time. Randall, the owner of the company, has gained the attention of a friend of yours. He's being watched, perhaps brought in for questioning right now. He'll talk to get off. He frigged up a sale of a very high-priced woman and promised your friends that she would be delivered and they would get over two million. He planned on being long gone out of here. But the problem is, he's already selling the company to this other individual."

"Why are you sharing this with me? I have no interest in their business."

"That's not what I heard. But then again, maybe you decided to step down and allow Nicolai Vollup to gain more power and finally knock you out of the black market deals that made you into the multimillionaire you are today."

Dom sat forward in his chair, his face becoming red in an instant.

"Are you telling me the truth?" he asked.

Warner handed over the thumb drive. On it contained enough evidence to make Dom want to eliminate his competition and destroy the man who had been diligently working behind his back to discredit him and destroy Dom's enterprise. All gathered and very quickly by Gemini and his friends who insisted upon helping Warner.

"What is on it?"

"What you need to know to come to an informed business decision. But remember, I was never here. I don't know a thing, and you don't know where you got that thumb drive. Got it?"

Dom smirked. "Take care, my friend. Enjoy retirement."

Warner nodded his head and exited the room, hoping that Dom trusted him enough to look at the thumb drive and connect the dots. Randall and the others were going down and they would all be destroyed. Now he had to wait to make sure that Nicolai was eliminated once and for all.

* * * *

Mercedes was in the supermarket along with Taylor. As he grabbed some cereal, she walked down the aisle to where the flowers were. She thought about Warner. It had been a week since he left and she was getting more and more worried about him. She looked at them and even their beauty didn't make her smile. She loved being with Kurt and Taylor, but it felt different not having Warner there, too. He completed them. They needed to be together all four of them.

As she headed back around the aisle, she saw a man walking toward her just as she saw Taylor come, too.

Their eyes locked and something came over her. She went to scream. The man grabbed her and Taylor yelled out, "Let go of her.

She watched as the man turned while Taylor rushed to her in uniform and the man pulled a gun and shot him.

She cried out in shock as she watched Taylor fall to the ground backward as the man drug her from the store.

She was kicking and screaming and as one of the clerks showed up nearby, the man shot at him. The kid ducked and she screamed as he pulled her out the exit door.

"Let go of me. I'm not going anywhere with you," she yelled but then there was another man and he smirked at her.

"Don't fight us, it will only make matters worse for you." She struggled to get free then felt the prick to her neck. She saw the needle and then felt the effects of what they gave her. She was shoved into the backseat of the dark sedan. They had her, and all she kept thinking about was Taylor and how he got shot. *Taylor is dead, because of me.*

* * * *

"What do you mean you guys lost the vehicle? That was our only way of finding her. Fuck!" Taylor yelled as he sat in a chair, no shirt on and a major bruise already forming on his chest.

"Thank God you were wearing that bulletproof vest."

"Yeah, real fucking good I was. The hit nearly knocked me out."

"Beats the other alternative," Max stated.

"We have to find them. She's dead if we don't," Taylor said, feeling sick and angry.

"Taylor." He looked up and saw Pinto, Warner's friend.

"We know where they took Mercedes."

"What?" both Taylor and Max replied. There were others around them, including Mike Spencer and Monroe and Caldwell Gordon.

"What do you need from us?" Caldwell asked, straight-faced.

"Warner said sit tight, he has a plan. Kurt is with him."

"Oh shit," Taylor said, knowing that this was a seriously dangerous situation and he could lose all three of them.

* * * *

"This is your fucking plan?" Kurt said to Warner as Warner rechecked his Glock and remained expressionless.

They were sitting in the woods right outside of the estate preparing to raid the place.

"Listen to me, Randall does not know that one of the key players who wants to take over his business has got a major enemy with ties in the area. Randall can't just sell this off to him without following protocol."

"You're talking about organized crime shit?"

"Even crazier fucking bastards. Russians and Ukrainians with bad blood between them."

"Oh fuck," Kurt said and ran his hands through his hair.

"Why are you involved with that? I mean how the hell do you know this shit?" Kurt asked.

"You've done jobs for different individuals just as I have over the years, Kurt. You know we've made connections. But after today I'm done. It's all so fucked up, and you never know who is telling the truth, who is setting you up, or when someone might just shoot you in the back. We need to get all loose ends tied so we're done forever. You, me, Taylor, and Mercedes can live normal lives and be together without worrying."

"We have permission for justified kills?" Kurt asked, holding his gun.

"These fuckers have our woman, there's nothing more justified than that."

"We have to get to Mercedes. God knows what they've done to her already."

"I know, and listen, when we get to her I'll explain the next step."

"What?"

"Let's move. I hate sitting around waiting."

* * * *

Mercedes was crying her head hurt so badly. She knew the tears were making it worse but she couldn't stop. She was scared. These men had tied her up to a bed, in a nice bedroom no less, and stripped her to her panties and bra. When she tried to resist they hit her and threatened her with guns.

She tried pulling her wrists from the restraints but she couldn't. They were too tight and chafed her skin.

She heard the door creak open and she swung her head to see who it was.

Two men. Men she didn't recognize at all. They wore suit pants, dress shirts, and ties. They looked like businessmen and then they spoke.

Was that Russian?

"This is her," the one guy said in broken English and waved a hand toward the bed. The taller, bulkier man moved forward.

"Better than the pictures you sent. You sure she is part of the deal?" the man asked as he moved closer and held her gaze. They had tied a piece of material over her mouth and gagged her. She felt like choking but her throat was dry.

He reached out his big hand and trailed a finger along her belly. She wiggled and tried pulling away but the ropes were tied tight to her ankles, too.

His finger grazed over her pussy and she felt sick. She prayed he didn't rape her but she knew better. If someone didn't rescue her she was as good as raped and dead. They were going to sell her.

He cupped her breasts. "Bigger than the pictures."

The other man approached and smiled.

"I know. A pleasant surprise. She is special in so many ways."

"Hmm. I suppose so."

He stared at her.

"You will be obedient and you will do as I say, and maybe you will live. Then I will decide if you will be all mine or if I can make better money selling you to my associates for their pleasure and make some cash." He ran his hands along her thighs then to her pussy.

"She is petite. Lots of men like that. I will accept her and the offer of the business, Randall. I will also take a taste and determine her fate with me."

He leaned closer and cupped her cheeks and chin.

So the other guy was Randall? He was the main operator of the business that abducted women and sold them. The slimy fucking bastard. If she got a chance she would kill him. But right now she was shaking. This man, the one saying that she was his, had a mean, nasty look in his eyes. She would rather die than be forced to have sex with him or anyone he chose. In fact, she would make him kill her. There was no way she would ever survive being raped by multiple men. Never.

"Get me the papers," the man said to Randall.

"Yes, Nicolai."

"I'm going to remove this gag. You can't be comfortable, and I want to hear your voice. The voice that will cry out in ecstasy as I make you come for the very first time, virgin," he said as he undid the gag.

"Fuck you," she spat at him the moment the material left her mouth. His eyes widened and darkened.

He sat up and then straddled her.

"Fuck me? I don't think so. You will obey," he said and began touching her, caressing her breasts as she fought the restraints. She was crying and screaming at him when he struck her across the mouth. She growled, feeling so very angry she thought if her hands were free she could kill him herself.

"Get away from me. I will never be yours."

"That's where you're wrong." He covered her mouth and kissed her, plunging his tongue between her teeth and lying all his weight on her body, crushing her.

She didn't know what to do. She was so desperate, so angry, she bit down on his tongue, hearing his roar instantly. He pounded on her body and she opened her mouth and cried out, releasing him, tasting the disgusting blood and his scent in her mouth and through her nostrils. She was sick and could vomit.

The sound of alarms blaring drew his attention toward the door.

He jumped up, cut the ropes, and grabbed her. He retied the ones behind her back as she struggled to breathe. She hurt everywhere.

He shoved her along with him as he drew a gun and looked out the door in the hallway. In the distance she heard shots being fired but couldn't be sure. What was going on?

She struggled to get free from his grasp. She rocked to the right and he yelled at her then shoved her head to the wall where there was a sharp sconce. It shattered against her temple and cheek. She felt the sting and the cut instantly. Her vision blurred and she no longer fought his hold as she feared falling on her face and losing consciousness. She was in the middle of some kind of war as bullets whizzed by her and what sounded like rapid gunfire echoed outside.

"This way, Nicolai. We have the truck ready," someone yelled. It was one of his guards.

As they headed down the next flight of stairs, she moaned in pain and felt like vomiting. Her head throbbed.

As he got to the end of the staircase, gripping her tight, she heard the yelling. She heard Randall say, "I give up. Don't kill me."

She saw two men in black and then an SUV with tinted windows.

Men got out the vehicles.

She didn't know what was going on and then Nicolai was pulling her back into the house and then shoving her into a room. He paced in front of her, looking like a wild animal. She was bleeding and all she wanted to do was lie down and sleep.

He jerked her toward him.

"You. This is your fault. It has to be." He struck her across the mouth and she fell to the floor.

"Get away from her now." She wasn't sure if she were imagining it or not, but she heard Kurt's voice and then saw him and Warner. They were dressed in black. Her vision blurred, her eyes closed, and then opened as she tried to remain conscious. She couldn't. She heard bits and pieces of the exchanged words. Did Warner know Nicolai?

"Get her out of here," Warner said to Kurt. She felt Kurt's arms go around her and scoop her up into his arms. In the distance she heard nothing. It was silent.

"Kurt?"

He said nothing. Maybe he grunted, cursed, complained about her injuries and wanted to kill. It was all mixed up. The words, her vision as she passed by a brick wall, heard a door slam, saw darkness, smelled woods then felt the cold seat beneath her and the scent of leather.

Then she heard two gunshots. The door closed.

"We've got you. You're safe now, Mercedes. We'll get you to the hospital just hold on."

A moment later a door opened and closed.

"Good?" she heard Kurt's voice ask.

"Good," Warner said and then she felt the motion of the car and her head throbbing, her belly aching before she lost consciousness in the safety of Kurt's arms.

Epilogue

Mercedes woke up in bed to the smell of soap, cologne, and she knew where she was. The safety of her men's home as she had been for the last several weeks.

They'd made her rest and catered to her every need. She was getting stronger and stronger, and each day she wanted to press for answers as to what had happened to Nicolai, and how Kurt and Warner knew how to find her. But then she would remember that conversation from a month ago. How Warner had explained that if they still did the jobs they had before meeting her that they could never tell her about them and she couldn't ask. She had a feeling that somehow Warner knew Nicolai and had been responsible for bringing down Randall's operation, ending the sick business the man had as well as ending Nicolai's life.

They thought she was sleeping, or so far gone when they were getting her medical help so they talked freely. Warner and Kurt. They mentioned doing the final job and being free, and how things worked out after all and how relieved they were that she was alive and they saved her.

She'd thought about that and realized that none of it mattered. She wasn't going to die. They'd saved her and she loved Taylor, Kurt, and Warner with all her heart.

"Hey, beautiful, you're awake," Taylor said, walking into the room.

She smiled softly.

"What time is it?"

"Who cares," he replied like he did every time she asked what time, what day, wanting her to just relax and heal and have no worries even about the simple things.

He brushed the hair from her cheeks and then tilted her chin to the side.

"The stitches are healing well. Dr. Anders knows a great plastic surgeon who can make sure there isn't any scarring," he said, and she swallowed hard.

"I want to get up and maybe walk around a little."

"Honey, you just took a bath a few hours ago. That's a lot in one day."

"No it isn't. You're babying me and I'm getting tired of it."

"Really?" she heard Kurt's voice and saw him standing in the doorway. She felt the sense of intimidation but desire overruled it. Her face burned.

"Where's Warner?"

"He's around," Kurt said and she wondered if her were lying to her. She had freaked out when they said he wasn't there when she first awoke in the hospital. Then, every day, she insisted they were nearby or she felt scared. It was silly, but she didn't want them taking any chances of getting hurt or worse killed. Maybe it was because she didn't know the intensity of their jobs before, but now was different. They were her men, her lovers, and she wanted to be with them forever.

"I want to see him," she said and then shoved down the sheets. She was only wearing a shirt. Taylor's deputy T-shirt. She felt the funny sensation after getting up too quickly and Kurt cursed.

"Easy, baby, damn it to hell. You can't be jumping around jerking your head like that. You're still recovering."

"I'm fine, Kurt. I need to move around or the aches and pains will be from nonuse and stiffness," she said, feeling a little better being up like this.

Kurt helped her and she pushed his hand away. He placed his hands on his hips.

"What's wrong?"

"Nothing," she replied with attitude.

She went to walk passed him.

"It doesn't sound like nothing." She jerked her head up to see Warner standing in the doorway, wearing only his jeans and no shirt. Her pussy clenched and she licked her lips.

"Someone in a bad mood?" he said to her. She crossed her arms in front of her chest.

"Where were you?" she asked. He raised one of his eyebrows at her and stepped closer.

"Around," he replied.

She released an annoyed sigh. "So this is how it's going to be? I'm on a need-to-know basis with everything. Because I'm sick of it. I accepted you and Kurt not telling me about everything that went down and whether you knew that Nicolai character or not. I accepted you telling me that I can't ask questions about your pasts, your jobs, and your capabilities. Fine. But when I want to know where my men are I don't expect to hear the word *around*. You got it?" she asked, raising her voice as her eyes filled with tears and her emotions got the better of her. She was scared. She was fragile in so many ways from the traumatic experience but mostly she was affected by the fact she finally let her guard down and learned to love these three men.

In a flash Warner was across the room and pulling her into his arms.

He lifted her up and pressed her up against the wall.

He cupped her cheeks and held her gaze.

"Taylor, Kurt, grab the lube and get everything ready. Our woman is getting a spanking and then she's going to get some loving the way our woman deserves."

He covered her mouth and kissed her and in no time at all she didn't remember why she'd gotten so mad at them, but only how much she loved them and needed them in her life forever. She dared to love them and would do so for the rest of her life, and they loved her back. Nothing else in the world mattered to her more than having the love and the protection of Taylor, Kurt, and Warner Dawn. Her men, her lovers, her rescuers, and her partners for life.

Then she felt that little bit of defiance vibrate within her as Warner placed her onto Taylor as he held his cock, waiting for her to ride him.

She took off her shirt and tossed it to the floor then rubbed her hands together.

"Finally you understand exactly what I want. The three of you inside of me," she said.

"Mercedes." The three of them said her name in warning and she giggled as they all touched her together, then loved her together. That was all she ever really wanted.

THE END

WWW.DIXIELYNNDWYER.COM

ABOUT THE AUTHOR

People seem to be more interested in my name than where I get my ideas for my stories from. So I might as well share the story behind my name with all my readers.

My momma was born and raised in New Orleans. At the age of twenty, she met and fell in love with an Irishman named Patrick Riley Dwyer. Needless to say, the family was a bit taken aback by this as they hoped she would marry a family friend. It was a modern day arranged marriage kind of thing and my momma downright refused.

Being that my momma's families were descendants of the original English speaking Southerners, they wanted the family blood line to stay pure. They were wealthy and my father's family was poor.

Despite attempts by my grandpapa to make Patrick leave and destroy the love between them, my parents married. They recently celebrated their sixtieth wedding anniversary.

I am one of six children born to Patrick and Lynn Dwyer. I am a combination of both Irish and a true Southern belle. With a name like Dixie Lynn Dwyer it's no wonder why people are curious about my name.

Just as my parents had a love story of their own, I grew up intrigued by the lifestyles of others. My imagination as well as my need to stray from the straight and narrow made me into the woman I am today.

Enjoy *Dare to Love* and allow your imagination to soar freely.

For all titles by Dixie Lynn Dwyer, please visit
www.bookstrand.com/dixie-lynn-dwyer

Siren Publishing, Inc.
www.SirenPublishing.com